IN THE SUN'S COLD HEART

The dipper ship sliced into the heavier layers of the photo-sphere at high speed. "Open collection cells," Matthew said. The cells were forty-eight percent full when a dark ring appeared on the detector display. "Coordinate this pattern. Go after it. Dive!"

The ring on the display shifted. With astonishing speed, the source of the emanation passed under the ship and raced away. Matthew screwed the ship in a murderous turn. The computer reported general failures of a dozen functions.

The source was rising toward them, hundreds of kilometers wide and shapeless. If Matthew could get close enough, he intended to fly into it and trap what portion he could in his collector cells. The target ring expanded to fill the display. Matthew nudged the ship forward and opened the cells.

A strange, cooling sensation ran over his skin. Gradually he noticed the normally dark control module was suffused with a clear blue light. He looked down and realized his fluorescing body was illuminating the module.

His extremities were ice cold, and his limbs trembled with increasing violence. He tried to speak, but the cold effluvium blocked his vocal cords . . .

SUNDIPPER

Paul B. Thompson

ST. MARTIN'S PRESS/NEW YORK

SUNDIPPER

Published by arrangement with the author.

Library of Congress Catalog Card Number: 87-50345

ISBN: 0-312-90706-0   Can. ISBN: 0-312-90707-9

Printed in the United States of America

First St. Martin's Press mass market edition/August 1987

10 9 8 7 6 5 4 3 2 1

To Sara
Q.E.D.

One never climbs so high as when he knows not where he is going.

—NAPOLEON BONAPARTE

CHAPTER 1

All men are born in darkness. Some more than once.

This man was motionless, half submerged in the milky gelatin that filled the glass box in which he lay. He was naked. His heart beat ten times a minute, and his breath came once every five heartbeats.

When his body temperature rose above that of the ambient air, sensors immersed in the gel activated the resuscitation system. Pure oxygen began to flow into his nostrils. A slender metal rod, tipped with a clear vial and microbore needle, dropped down from the overhead array. Below the needle was a polished metal ball. The ball rolled over the man's skin, up his breastbone to the base of his neck. Ultrasonic waves mapped the trachea and esophagus, the veins and lymph nodes. When the ball found the carotid artery, it stopped. The needle passed through epidermis, dermis, and the artery wall. The vial pumped twelve milliliters of stimulant into the man's bloodstream.

His hands knotted. Knees and elbows tightened. The muscles in his back and shoulders contracted, drawing his head back deeper into the gel. He thrashed and kicked for several seconds, but the gel buffered the violence of his awakening.

The spasms passed. The man sat up. He opened his eyes and looked down at himself. From head to toe he was burnt copper brown.

"Hell," he muttered.

He wiped cold goo from his neck and blew the excess from his ears. The chronograph on the wall showed 14:12 hours. Early afternoon on Earth.

"Hello?" called the man. His slimy feet touched the carpeted floor. "Where the hell am I?"

The lights overhead brightened from their twilight mode. A cultured, well-modulated voice issued from the walls: "Good morning, Mr. Lawton."

"It's afternoon."

"So it is. Are you properly oriented now, sir?"

"Yeah. I'm at home, right? You're the house audion."

"Exactly," said the house. "How was your recovery?"

"Rough. How much Sting did you give me?"

"Twelve milliliters, sir."

"Twelve! No wonder I feel like I've been dropped on my head. You shouldn't ever give me more than ten cc's," he said.

"Begging your pardon, sir, but the medical chip says you received some ten milliliters of Crux before being sent back from space. To revive you properly required a large dose of stimulant."

Lawton yawned. His jaw popped ominously from the effort. "Did my load reach Island Omicron?" he asked.

"It did, sir. I am informed by the banking audion in Atlanta that eleven point seven megalots have been credited to your account," said the house.

Eleven million, seven hundred thousand. A damn good

payoff, though Lawton had hoped to breach the twelve-megalot mark this time. Maybe next quarter.

He said, "What's it like outside?"

"It is raining, sir. Air temp is seventeen degrees Celsius, humidity is ninety-eight percent, and the wind is from the south at sixteen kph."

Rain. Cool, delicious moisture falling from the sky. Lawton left the recovery room and walked through the silent house. He parted the plexi doors and went out on the deck.

Gray clouds clung closely to Buncombe Horse Range Ridge, obscuring any view of the valley below. Lawton's house was fixed in the hard stone of the south slope, 1,464 meters above sea level. The only other dwelling in the area was a second mountainside retreat, thirty-five meters east and slightly above his place. Since Lawton had bought his house in the Black Mountains, he had never seen anyone in the upper house.

The rain fell lazily in big drops. Lawton stood in it, jaw slack, soaking in the delightful chill it brought. Bits of gel washed loose from his hair and slid down his chest. He remained like this a long time.

The wind swirled around him, gusting hard from the west. Lawton opened his eyes. In his rainy reverie, he had half turned and was facing the neighboring house.

There was a woman standing on her own deck, looking down at the burned and naked man. Lawton was more surprised than embarrassed, and he stared at her. The wind drove rain into his eyes, and when he had rubbed them clear again the woman was gone.

Matthew Lawton was a sundipper. In the entire solar system, no more than two dozen men and women did what he did, and by mutual agreement he was the best.

It was a simple job, really: flying a specially made energy-collecting spacecraft to the sun. The dipper flew through the corona and chromosphere to the relatively cool surface of the photosphere, 6,100 degrees Celsius cool.

Collecting cells in the dipper's ship absorbed all varieties of energy—heat, light, gravity, tidal force—and converted them to high-intensity plasma. Banks of accumulators, sheathed in delicate magnetic "bottles," held the energy until it could be transferred to purchasers waiting in Mercury orbit. The chief customers of the sundippers were the eight Transaster space colonies orbiting between Earth and Mars. The colonies relied on the dippers for 30 percent of their domestic power needs and 85 percent of their industrial requirements. They paid very well indeed for their little packets of the sun. They had little choice. Neither satellites nor passive solar panels could match the speed and massive outpouring of power a sundipper could provide.

Simple. Fly a ship, shaped like a curved disc seventy meters in diameter, into one of the hottest fires in the galaxy. Alone. Sealed in a totally dark, totally silent, heat-shedding module, necessarily blinded to the inferno outside. Guide the craft entirely by instruments, avoiding prominences and spicules; hoping and praying to assorted archaic deities that the instruments held out (the failure rate was generally 65 percent), and that you weren't engulfed by an erupting solar flare.

Murderous gravity. Radiation so intense it cooked you brown, even through layers of shielding thick enough to smother a plasma blast. No communications were possible through the storm of raging hydrogen ions. A dipper went in alone, did his job alone, and often died alone.

Many insisted it was too dangerous. "It ought to be done by robot ships," they said. Never. Robots and audions were capable of guiding the ships, but a machine could never make inspired decisions. This had been proven years before. One colony, Sky Island Alpha, built an experimental audion-controlled dipper. It returned with an eleven percent load. The Transasters tried again. Nine percent. The audion was too smart to succeed. It would not risk itself or the ship in hazardous maneuvers. Only a human being would gamble his or her life for profit. Only a few, very special humans.

Of the intimate in-group of sundippers, Matthew Lawton was the senior member. All those who came before him were either dead or retired. Most were dead.

He was known as Old Hundred Percent because he never flaked (left the photosphere) without completely filling his cells.

Old Hundred Percent was twenty-nine years old.

His hair had once been brown. Now it was white. He dipped less frequently than he once had. For every three quarters of idle luxury he spent on Earth, he spent one quarter dipping. Any more often was self-destructively greedy. In his youth (so long ago!) he dipped a quarter on, a quarter off. By the time he was twenty-five, Matthew was the richest noncorporate resident of the Western Hemisphere.

He cut back his dipping, but he couldn't quit. If he had earned nothing but his bed and bread, Matthew would have continued to dip the sun. He was addicted to the challenge, the danger. There was also the Gift.

Fresh from the water jet, Matthew wrapped himself in a robe and sauntered to the kitchen. His stomach was a gaping crevasse, for he had not eaten solid food in two weeks.

"What would you like, sir?" asked the house.

"Coffee," Matthew said. "Three eggs; no, four. Scrambled in butter. What kind of meat's on hand?"

"Real or reconstituted?"

"Real."

"Pork loin, six kilograms. Chicken, eight kilograms.

Lamb, point eight kilograms. Beef, twelve kilograms. Shrimp—"

"Stop. I want two filet mignons, well done, with onions and mushrooms, and three hundred grams of glâce d'or," he said.

"Excessive protein intake is not advisable after prolonged subsistence on synthetics."

"Who are you, my mother? Fix what I tell you," Matthew snapped. In silent obedience, eggs appeared from the refrigerator, and two dark red filets dropped on the grill.

Matthew went to the living room. He poured himself a half-liter of wine and saluted his reflection in the transparent doors. It was night.

He slowly sipped the Chardonnay. The trickle of wine sent his empty stomach into painful spasms. Rather than stop, Matthew gulped down the whole glass. If he could keep it down, he'd be all right. Alcohol soothed post-Crux cramps.

He gagged and dropped the glass. Matthew threw back the door and ran to the deck railing. Better to be sick on the mountain than on the rug. Nausea climbed his throat seeking an exit. He clenched his teeth and fought it down.

You will not be sick! he thought furiously. Think how much this wine cost!

He put his back to the rail as the sickness faded. The exterior lights of the next house caught his eye. A large private skimmer was parked on the roof. Figures moved across the lighted windows. The woman was not alone.

Eggs were steaming on his plate when Matthew returned. "Who's in the neighbor's house?" he asked loudly.

"Checking," said the audion. "The lessee is one S. Mackensen." One of its manipulators flipped Matthew's steaks. Another stirred a sauté pan full of sliced yellow onions and button mushrooms.

"Man or woman?" asked Matthew through a forkful of egg.

"No indication of gender is given on the lease. Shall I endeavor to find out, sir?"

"Yeah, call their audion and ask it." Coffee, filets, and vegetables were relayed to the table. Matthew ate every bit. He was starting on the glâce d'or when the audion reported on its efforts.

"I am sorry to say, sir, that the audion in the next dwelling has been altered," it said with obvious distaste.

"What do you mean?"

"I mean, sir, it no longer speaks."

"So?" said Matthew. "Try card-linking."

"I did. The internal system has been isolated, and will not accept any external access."

"Sounds like S. Mackensen wants a lot of privacy."

The audion replied, "It is very bad form to alter a domestic audion in such a manner. If I were you, sir, I would snub these people."

"You're not me," Matthew reminded it. He stood. "I'm through. Clean up."

In the bedroom, Matthew shrugged off his robe and slippers. The big oval bed seemed cold and uninviting without Sian. He ought to call her.

The request panel chimed. "Make a link to Sian Donnelly," he said. "Tell her Matt is home, alone, and needs her very much." The audion acknowledged and sent the message.

CHAPTER 2

Skulking in the umbra of Mercury, like a thief in the shadows, is the base of operations of the sundippers. This spindly construct, called Icecube by its residents, is home and haven for the twenty-odd ships engaged in the trade. Icecube is unique in the solar system in that it was built and maintained by private funds. The dippers, mechanics, and station staff hold corporate title over Icecube. The shares are frequently reapportioned according to seniority as associated members—usually the pilots—die.

Matthew Lawton first saw Icecube from the viewpoint of the Lunarian freighter *Collins,* on which he served as Cargo Handler, Fourth Class. At nineteen he left Tranquility University on Luna, unwilling to pursue either of his parents' professions of engineering or civil service. At twenty he signed on the *Collins* and began the inner circuit of the solar system, visiting the cloud platforms of Venera-Vostok; the defense stations *Australia, Antarctica,* and *Pacific;* and ultimately, Icecube.

It was his intention to jump ship in Mercury orbit, a resolution made easier by the difficult passage he had had on the *Collins*. The captain of the freighter, First Guide Alverado, was indifferent to the plight of the crew. The ordinary men of the *Collins,* of whom Matthew was the lowest of the low, suffered from harassment and abuse by the junior officers. Matthew's personal nemesis was Cargo Chief Muñez. Muñez never let him get away with doing the most insignificant task once; five to ten times was his usual demand. All that kept Matthew's considerable temper in check was the knowledge he would soon be saying *adios* to the miserable *Collins*.

The freighter had only two hours to unload supplies at Icecube. Matthew walked his lift augmenter through the cargo bay with a thousand kilos of ships' parts under his arm. He set the goods down in the storage area on the space station and abandoned the machine. He hid among the crates and tore the *Collins* flash from his sleeve. As he hoped, Alverado did not delay departure to look for him. The *Collins* flew away, and Matthew was free.

Free, but unemployed. There was plenty of demand for dippers, but becoming one required several hard-to-come-by items. First, a ship. Sundippers—the ships—are one-off craft, totally unlike any other class of space vehicle. They are large, single-pilot ships, shaped like discs or ovals. The underside is studded with energy-collecting plates. The hull is packed with storage cells. In the dynamic center of the ship is the control module, a pod-shaped housing where the pilot sits.

Sundippers must have aerodynamic surfaces in order to maneuver in the dense photosphere. A proper balance must be struck between strength and lightness. A heavy ship would require a large engine (expensive) and would be hard to handle in the violent currents within the sun. Yet strength is essential for pulling away from the massive gravity. The single most frequent cause of fatal accidents is structural failure during the exit phase.

Besides lacking a ship, Matthew had no berthing privileges, no buying connections with the Transasters, and no experience at all.

Working dippers laughed at him when he asked for information. The permanent Icecube staff was coldly condescending. It wasn't unusual for young men and women to show up in the station, clutching fanciful notions about becoming dippers. It was so romantic! So exciting! And the money—well, why didn't everyone do it?

The dreamers learned fast. The survival rate for a *trained* pilot after four dips was 85 percent. After eight dips, this dropped to 60 percent. By the time twelve plunges into the sun had been made, the survival rate was 31 percent. Less skillful pilots never got that far. The average number of dips done before death was seven and a half. The mean age of dead dippers was twenty-three.

After ten days of being ignored, Matthew was so discouraged he would have reboarded the *Collins* had it been there. In fact, he had no way off Icecube until the next transport arrived. Rather than starve, he fell back on a resource he had utilized extensively in college.

Despite the ubiquity of holoid games and technotronic entertainment, cards were still the premier form of gambling wherever humanity dwelt. Matthew established himself in Icecube's large lounge with a deck of cards and played poker to feed himself. He soon discovered he could do far better than mere subsistence.

Idle dippers were addicted to gambling. Other popular diversions were drugs, drinking, and joyflights. There was sex, too; one dipper in three was female. But with money being made by the megalot every hour—hot money—it had to be passed along in order to cool.

In five days of concentrated playing, Matthew made fifty kilolots, ten times his quarterly salary on the *Collins*. He relieved every dipper he played against of credit chips except one. One man held his own.

He was very tall—198 cm—and desperately thin. His skin was so deeply colored by the invidious radiation he resembled a mahogany statue. The tall man's scalp was covered by a thin stubble of white hair.

The man won a fair pot from Matthew. Vexed, the younger man said, "What's your name, Pro?"

"Jack Sangamon," he replied. "Independent Collector Eight-Eight." Matthew was impressed. In his short time on Icecube he had learned the lower a dipper's number, the greater his seniority. Jack Sangamon was the first one he had met with a number under one hundred. He looked old. His age, Jack said, was thirty-six. Matthew heard rumors later that Jack was over forty.

"Save the intros," said the dipper on Sangamon's left. "Deal the damn cards!"

The complainer's name was Vender. He was an old-timer, too—nearly thirty. Like most Transasters in the business, his was a "working name."

Sangamon dealt seven-card stud, high-low. Matthew received a pair of nines in the hole and a low spade showing. Sangamon showed a red three. Vender had an ace.

After a few rounds the other players dropped out. Only Matthew, Sangamon, and Vender remained. Matthew was going for high, as he had three nines. Vender and Sangamon were apparently battling for low, and the tall man was losing.

Matthew bumped every bet, confident he had half the pot no matter who won low. Sangamon had 3-7-6-2 up. Vender showed A-4-3-5. All he needed was a deuce in the hole to have a perfect low.

Sangamon was cool, never raising, never checking. He kept up with Matthew's incessant raises until almost twenty kilolots lay on the table.

The last card went down. Matthew drew trash. His nines seemed like a lock on high. His ace-nine upcards gave him the first bet in the last round.

He marked a chip. "One kilolot," he said. Vender stared at him.

"Damn capper," he said, tossing in his matching bet. Sangamon marked his responding wager.

"Make it five K," he said calmly. A ripple of astonishment circled the lounge. People gathered around the table.

Matthew bit his lip. Vender had the best low in sight. Could Sangamon be going for high after all? Three of his upcards were hearts. Had he filled a flush?

He met the raise. Vender put his last chip in and called.

Now they had to declare. In front of each player, under the edge of the table, was a touch panel. Pressing the panel once made a green light blink on top. That meant low. Two presses for a red light; that meant high. Three presses for both lights, which meant the player was opting for high and low.

Matthew's finger strayed to the panel. He pushed once, prepared for a second, then stopped. Something he saw in Vender's face changed his mind. Matthew went low.

Vender went high.

Sangamon declared for both. To win, he had to win both.

Matthew displayed a garbage arrangement by tossing his pair. He was left with A-4-7-9-10 as low. Vender saw Matthew's cards and muttered a curse. He turned over two more aces, giving him three in all.

Sangamon had the flush and won high. His low was 2-3-6-7-9. He beat out Matthew and won the entire pot.

Onlookers applauded. Vender swept his cards off the table and stalked away. Sangamon had taken fifteen kilolots from him in one hand. He got a similar amount from Matthew.

The crowd dispersed. "That was a hell of a hand," said Matthew.

"I've had better," said Sangamon genially. "I once took thirty-two K off a First Guide on Island Iota. We were playing double-red, and he had to match the pot or drop out. He doubled it, and I won on the next card." Sangamon signaled for drinks. A carafe of *E*-vodka ("Distilled in Space: 120 Proof") arrived, and the older man poured Matthew a generous portion.

"Thank you, Pro Sangamon," he said.

"Jack."

"'A cure for dust,'" said Matthew, using a Lunarian toast.

"*Skoal*," replied Jack.

They talked for a while. Matthew revealed his frustrated ambition to be a dipper. Jack sucked air through his teeth and slowly turned his glass between his fingers.

"You don't want to be a dipper," he said. "Oh, you got the nerve and the brains, but it's a desperate business, boy. Go back to school."

"I won't. I may have to go back to intrasystem freighters, but I won't go back to Luna!"

"All right. What'll you give me if I can fix it so you get a try at dipping?" said Jack.

"What do you want?"

"Money and a favor."

"How much money?"

"Ten K ought to cover it," said Jack. Matthew handed him a chip for that amount.

"What about the favor?"

"Later. I don't know what it'll be yet," said Jack.

Matthew wondered if the skinburnt man was joking. Jack was quite sober.

He took Matthew to see one of the fleet managers. Dippers were divided into independents and fleet pilots. Three ex-dippers had set themselves up as fleet operators. They hired pilots, paid them off, and kept the remaining profit for themselves. It was a lucrative arrangement, and far less dangerous than dipping personally. The three managers were Amram Bentick, Wellington Yu, and the legendary Rainbow Harvester.

It was Yu that Jack took Matthew to meet. Yu was an East Hemian from Hong Kong. He moved about Icecube in a mobile chair. Matthew first thought Yu was lazy, as he was very fat, but on closer inspection he saw the man had no legs.

"Greetings, my Pro," said Jack with a touch of mockery. The fat man pivoted his chair toward Sangamon. Neither man offered to shake hands.

"The ever-rancid Sangamon," Yu said. "Why do you offend my eyes with your presence?"

"I want you to meet someone. Matthew Lawton, this is Wellington Yu. Yu, this is Matthew Lawton, late of Luna."

Yu folded his hands across his belly. "Well?" he said.

"I want you to make Lawton a sundipper," said Jack.

"He's just a boy."

"So were we once. I think he'll make it if he gets the right training. You can do that. Ernesto hasn't come back from Mars, has he? You don't have anyone to fly the *Ki-Lin.*"

"I expect Ernesto any day now," said Yu.

"He's not coming back. He funked his last dip. His nerve's broken, and he won't ever come near Icecube or you again," said Jack.

Yu looked up at Matthew. "Can you fly, boy?"

"I have a Class 3 license," said Matthew.

"Ho, ho! So you can bounce pogos up and down. That's not piloting, boy." He said to Sangamon, "I can't use him."

"You'll use him. I have debt markers from you that are two quarters old. If I complain loud enough, maybe the Concordat Space Service will impound your ships till you pay me off," said Jack.

"Extortion comes easily to you, Sangamon. I almost believe you, but you don't want the Service probing into dipper accounts any more than I do. Where probes go, regulations follow."

"What difference does it make to me? I've got enough to retire on. I can sic the Service on you and go home a very rich man. It won't matter to me what happens out here once I'm comfortably set in Melbourne."

Yu's face showed the pressure Sangamon exerted was not to be denied. The crippled man had one last card to play.

"I will train him and put him in the *Ki-Lin,* if you cancel all my debts to you," he said.

Now it was Jack's turn to grimace. "Half the debt," said Jack.

"All."

Sangamon scratched his cocoa-colored cheek. "What the hell. It's only money. I *do* hate giving up my hold over you," he said. Yu smiled. Matthew thought he looked remarkably like the Great Buddha of Tycho Basin.

"I will have my audion scribe a chip for you," said Yu. He pointed a pudgy finger at Matthew. "You are now a valuable property, boy. If you disappoint me, I shall personally deliver your wretched body to ugly Sangamon for ill treatment." Yu spun around 180 degrees and rolled away.

"Thank you, Jack," Matthew said.

"Never mind, mate. Just be the best damned dipper that ever was. You're surely the most expensive student in history."

"How much did Yu owe you?"

Jack put a hand on Matthew's shoulder. "Six point two megalots," he said.

Matthew was staggered. "That's a fortune!" he exclaimed.

"The proceeds of one good dip," said Jack. "I'll earn twice that this quarter."

They walked back to the ship service shop. A strange inconsistency struck Matthew.

"Say, Jack; why did you ask me for ten kilolots, when you gave up six point two million for me a few minutes later?" he said.

"The sum meant a lot to you, didn't it?"

"It's about half of what's left of my poker winnings."

"I wanted to see how much of a sacrifice you were willing to make," said Jack.

"I'd have given it all," said Matthew. Jack nodded. They came to the corridor below the eighth pylon. Jack's ship, *Red Jack*, was moored there.

"Time to recheck the helium pump," he said. "See you around, Matt."

"Could I see inside your ship?"

"No," Jack said firmly. "No one goes on *Red Jack* but me."

"Why's that?"

"Safety. Independents have too many 'accidents.'"

Matthew watched Jack disappear down the corridor, ducking periodically to avoid projecting fixtures. He returned to the lounge. This time he played solitaire.

CHAPTER 3

A glorious morning dawned in the Atlantic District, and even Matthew could not hate the sun today.

He spent his first morning awake doing nothing. He reclined in a chaise on the deck, carefully sited so he could see the house of S. Mackensen. With a steady supply of white wine and the musicon playing Sibelius, he settled in for a restful day.

About 10:00 two figures appeared on the roof next door. The man and woman walked together to the expensive skimmer (a Magdeburg—too bulky for Matthew's tastes). After a few moments' conversation, the man kissed the woman pristinely on the cheek and climbed into his vehicle. The skimmer rose a few meters and rotated ninety degrees to face north. It lumbered away, its repulsor pattern kicking up a whirlwind of dust beneath it. The cloud of grit swept over Matthew's house, ruining his drink and getting into his eyes. He jumped up and cursed the fast receding skimmer.

The dust settled, Matthew looked back. The woman, clad in a bright blue kimono, was gazing down at him. He waved. She turned away and went inside.

Sian called after lunch. She was in the Triangle, but promised to come that evening. Matthew could not read the changes in her voice. She was eager to be with him, but there was a tautness in her tone he hadn't heard before. They had been apart 255 days. Much could change in that time.

By midafternoon Matthew had worked up enough gall to call his mysterious neighbor. The telaudion chimed twice. The connection was made with sound only; the holoid cube remained dark.

"Hello?" said a feminine voice.

"Yes, hello. Is this S. Mackensen?" said Matthew.

"Who is calling?"

"My name is Matthew Lawton. I'm your neighbor down the hill. We shared some dust this morning."

"I saw you." Talkative woman. He pressed on.

"I wanted to apologize for my appearance yesterday. I'd just come back from a deep space journey, and my medication hadn't quite worn off. I hope I didn't startle you," he said.

"You did not."

"I didn't know anyone was living up there," Matthew continued lamely.

"I didn't know anyone was living below," replied S. Mackensen.

"As long as we're neighbors, we might as well be sociable. Perhaps you'd care to come over for a drink some time."

"No." Talkative *and* polite.

"If I've offended you in some way . . ."

"I am not offended, Mr. Lawton. I came here to be alone, and my health does not permit me to make visits out of the house," she said.

"Should you change your mind, I'll be here. Call anytime," said Matthew.

"Thank you, but it seems doubtful I will. Good-bye." The connection ended.

Matthew was not used to being turned down so flatly. What was her problem? Her health hadn't prevented her from having an overnight visitor—a very friendly overnight visitor. Matthew puzzled and fumed over this paradox for hours, right up to the moment Sian's skimmer arrived.

The horizon was red when Sian ghosted in for a landing on Matthew's roof. She flew the machine herself, without audion aid, and she was good at it. The skimmer settled silently inside the painted circle. Sian switched off the repulsor circuits and pulled the com-mike from her head. The glow of the dash highlighted her face dramatically. Matthew felt a surprisingly sharp pang of desire.

"Darling," she said as they embraced. She pulled back and added, "You're so dark!"

"It's been a rough season, the height of the sunspot cycle," said Matthew. He held her closely and inhaled the marvelous fragrance of her skin. "Come on. Have you eaten yet?"

"No! When work was finished, I jumped in the skimmer and flew here," said Sian.

"Then I'll cook for you myself. No audion." She smiled and took his hand.

Sian sat on the counter as Matthew prepared dinner. Spacer-style Ad-bans were in vogue as casual wear, and she wore the tight wrappings well. It was all Matthew could do to concentrate on peeling the potatoes with her so near.

Sian was Matthew's age, though she looked much younger. This quarter her hair was tinted auburn (last time he saw her she'd been blonde), and her eyes were dyed violet.

"How's the Photech Corporation?" he said, slicing the potatoes into french fries.

"Same old foot-dragging mentality," she said. "Production's off, and everyone's ducking responsibility. No one wants to make the hard decisions. But that's going to change soon."

"Oh?"

"Yes. I've joined the Party."

Matthew stopped cutting. "You did what?" he said.

"I joined the Beneficial Party," said Sian. "It'll help me get ahead, Matt. I want to bring Party ideals and Earth-pride to the corporation."

"Sian, you know damn well what the Party does to companies once its members get inside. Confiscation. Redistribution."

She said, "It's called Beneficiation. It's for the good of all."

Matthew said nothing. He dumped the potatoes in a cooking pouch.

"It's never good when individual rights are sacrificed," he said slowly.

"You talk like one of the old Impatients. The myth of personal choice was refuted long ago, Matt. Don't you remember the Crisis?"

"I don't need a history lesson from the Party textchip. Besides being wrong, it's boring."

"I don't understand your attitude," said Sian. "You act as if the BP is some sort of ancient dictatorship, when it's done more for human happiness than any political group in history."

"At the expense of freedom?" said Matthew with heat.

"Freedom? What freedom? Can't people say and do what they want? Live where they want? Is there any crime, unemployment, pollution, or war?"

"Is that why they take over private companies, and send dissident thinkers to the Bast gasworks?"

Sian put out her chin and said primly, "Some people cannot accept progress."

Matthew slammed the pouch to the floor. He grabbed Sian's arm and dragged her from the counter. She struggled and protested all the way to the bathroom.

Matthew held her forcefully in front of the mirror. "What do you see?" he said.

"Your face and mine. Let me go, Matt—"

"What's on your face?" he said sharply. Sian wouldn't look. "What's on your face?" he demanded.

"You know what it is!" she said, turning away. He seized her chin and twisted her face to the glass. Under the sunlike Teblights, a series of letters and numbers were visible on Sian's left cheek.

"You're marked," said Matthew. "Every day, anywhere there are U-V rays, people see these marks and know who and what you are. Look at my face. Am I stencilled, like some bureaucrat's property?"

"You're a spacer. You don't have to be marked," she said. A single tear ran across the double row of tatoos: WH4FC 218.529.647.011.

"The 'Beneficial' Party did this to you, Shy. Sure, they let you move and make money and fuck whoever you want. Allow those things and ninety-nine percent of the world is satisfied. But when was the last time you did anything that counted? That made a difference in the world?"

"I contribute. I work hard at Photech."

"You contribute drivel. Pablum for the brain. An audion could do your job," he said.

Sian closed her eyes and shook with anger. "Damn you, Matt. I came here to be happy. Why do you have to be such a shit?" she said between sobs.

"I hate seeing you become part of that human ant hill. I know what happens to young execs who join. Remember my brother Simon? They ruined him. Made him into a spy against his own employers. Is that what you want to be?"

"It's easy for you to be virtuous! Try and keep up a decent appearance on three kilolots a month! You're rich. I want to be rich too. I want an audion house, a good skimmer, and to make trips off-world."

When she put it like that, Matthew hesitated. Wanting more and better was something he could understand. At least her interest in politics was pragmatic, not doctrinaire.

He slackened his grip. Sian turned in his arms to face him.

"Forget it, Shy," he said. "I had a rotten quarter out there. I fell apart. Can you believe it? The pale boys at Icecube held me down and sedated me." She held him tightly, and he whispered in her ear: "If I lose my mind, I don't know what'll happen."

"You're just tired, Matt," she said, stroking the back of his neck. "You need to forget about death and fire for a while."

"Any suggestions how?"

"Let the audion finish dinner," said Sian. "That'll keep it busy for an hour or two."

He kissed her once, and felt the contours of her body mold into his own. He was about to repeat himself when she put a hand to his mouth.

"Are you sure you can stand to make love to a Party member?" she said.

"I'll close my eyes," said Matthew.

"Independent Collector Two-Three-One requesting exit vector."

"Two-Three-One, you are passed to exit on vector Oh-Four-Four. Log course and ERT."

Matthew flashed the information to the repeater display on Icecube. "My course will be D-eight-eight parabolic retrograde. Estimated Return Time, seventeen point seventy-five hours," he said.

"The Fire Lane opens in eleven minutes. Have a good dip," said the Icecube controller.

"I always do," he replied.

His ship warped free of the station pylon. Matthew coasted through the cone of darkness behind Mercury as he adjusted his audion. "How do you feel?" he said.

"Quite well, thank you," it replied.

"Let's go scrape the sun," said Matthew.

Once the ship was clear of the penumbra, the instruments began registering the massive output of the sun. Heat. Ions. Gravity. Magnetic fountains. Uncountable rads of radiation.

"Fuel flow positive. Coolant active. Reserve capacity twenty-two percent," said the audion.

"Right. I want a constant watch on the tidal force meter," said Matthew. "If it goes to Red ten, yell. I don't care what I'm saying or doing, you interrupt me. Got that?"

"Yes, sir."

The bright side of Mercury unspooled beneath him. He opened a band and called the Fire Lane projector.

"Hello, Fire Truck; can you hear me? This is IC-Two-Three-One. Respond OTB," he said.

"Fire Truck here. Better hurry, Lawton. The Lane opens in four minutes."

"I'll be there."

Fire Truck came into view. The immense mobile projector covered more than a square kilometer of Mercurian real estate. Most of its surface area was taken up with solar panels, which provided power for the magnetic field generator. The truck crept eastward on enormous caterpillar treads, just fast enough to counter Mercury's rotation.

"I have you in sight," said Matthew.

"Ninety seconds," said the Truck operator.

Matthew tightened his seat grips. He had to penetrate the corona and chromosphere while the Lane was open. This meant accelerating hard, straight at the sun.

"Lane open! I say again, Lane open!" announced the operator.

"Straighto. Dipping now."

His ship flashed into the invisible Fire Lane. Only the silent gauges showed that the tunnel was there, protecting Matthew.

Mercury faded fast behind. Upon entering the Lane, all com-band communications were lost. If anything happened to Matthew now, no one could do anything to help him.

The ship gained speed as it curved in toward the sun. Matthew pushed a chip into the musicon. The opening notes of the *Eroica* Symphony resounded. Beethoven filled the module, and Matthew drew strength from it. He was not alone. The Vienna Philharmonic was with him.

"Contact with the photosphere in seven seconds," said the audion. "Circuit buffers engaged. Collection cells open."

Matthew fidgeted with the controls of the collection array. "Rig cells for overflow feed," he said. Instead of filling each cell individually, he was linking them, so that excess energy would spill over from full blocks to empty ones. It was a faster process, but riskier. If a surge developed, the whole array might overcharge.

Eroica thundered on, *allegro con brio*. The photosphere, undampened by the Fire Lane, overwhelmed the instruments. Matthew switched them off. Only the audion could see beyond the shell of the ship now.

Vibrations echoed through the hull. "Tidal force?" asked Matthew.

"Red seven, fluctuating to Red nine."

He angled the ship forty-five degrees to the surface of

the sun to decrease the buffeting. The ride smoothed out, but collection efficiency dropped. At the current rate, Matthew would exit the photosphere with only a 60 percent load.

Heat on the exterior of the ship was above six thousand degrees Kelvin. Behind his shells of metal, plexi, liquid helium, and electrostatic dissipators, Matthew sweated. He could feel the dip going wrong. The usual kick, the tingle up the spine and in the groin, was missing.

The ship shook with every pulse of the sun's core. Matthew put the aspect over to ninety degrees. He was flying edge-on. Collector efficiency dropped to barely thirty percent.

"T-force jumping, Red nine to Red ten," said the audion calmly.

"Compensate!" said Matthew. The ship shivered as if struck. "What was that?"

"Temp variations have caused power cells on the starboard site to rupture."

"Shut down. Shut them all down!"

"Feed flow is fused in the open position. Shall I jettison the array?" asked the audion.

"Me jettison? I'll flake first! Set a tangential course out—" The ship yawed violently. Matthew knew without asking that cells were bursting. The explosions moved inward, coming steadily toward him. When they reached the pilot's module, his heat shielding would be destroyed.

Panic gripped him. He didn't want to die. He didn't want to burn.

"Take us out!" he pleaded. The audion could not answer. Rupturing cells had severed its higher intelligence functions. Without the audion's control, the ship flipped over. It spiraled down, corkscrewing in to the sun's center.

Matthew jabbed the Crux ampule into his leg. It broke and cut his hand. There was no drug in it.

The walls around him glowed white. Metal sublimated into gas. Matthew put out his hand to hold the seams closed. His hand dissolved in a cloud of vaprous metal.

"Gem!" he cried. "Help me!"

A light came on.

Sian touched cool fingers to Matthew's face. "It's all right, darling. You've had a nightmare," she said.

He threw back the cover in disgust. The sheets were soaked with his sweat. Matthew went to the bathroom to wash the film of fear from his skin.

Sian brushed hair from her eyes and stared at the trail of white fluff leading from the bed to the door. Matthew had torn one of his genuine duck-down pillows to shreds.

"Matt," she called. "Who's Gem?"

From the bathroom came only the sound of running water.

CHAPTER 4

In his entire career Matthew Lawton crashed only one ship, and that one was not his.

His first four quarters as a dipper were very profitable for his boss, Wellington Yu. Matthew developed the habit of returning with a full load from every dip. This earned him a bonus and the promise from Yu of a better ship. His current craft, the *Ki-Lin,* was one of the last of the old-style chi ships. The collection array was carried at the tips of the intersecting fuselage, giving the *Ki-Lin* a comparatively small absorption area.

Matthew was returning from his sixth dip. He was flying down the Fire Lane when his motion sensor picked up another ship circling the Fire Truck. As he left the magnetic tunnel, his com-band came on.

"I don't have the facilities to handle your problem," the Truck operator was saying.

"What can I do?" asked the circling dipper. The Truck operator was conspicuously silent.

"This is Yu Group ship *Ki-Lin;* Matthew Lawton, pilot. What's going on?" he said.

"*Ki-Lin,* proceed on course two-five-five," ordered the Truck operator.

"Hey, wait. I need help!"

"Who's that?" asked Matthew.

"Gem Goldshield, Independent Collector Two--Oh-Nine, in the *Tourmaline.* I have a severe helium leak."

"This is none of your business, Lawton. Go back to Icecube," said the Fire Truck man.

"Blow off," he retorted. "Hello, Goldshield? How's your fuel situation?"

"I still have positive flow, but when the coolant's gone, the turbine pump is bound to fail."

"Undoubtedly; now listen: you're going to have to set your ship down. Try and get as far as the Sundown Zone before you ditch," he said.

"I understand," said Gem.

"I'll follow you in," said Matthew. "Set course due west. I'll stay with you."

"Are you crazy, Lawton? What's she gonna use for landing gear? If she cracks up on the surface, the power cells will flash her to ash before you can say 'Wellington Yu.'" The Truck operator worked for Yu, too, which explained his concern—at least for the *Ki-Lin* and its precious load.

The *Tourmaline* flew west, with the *Ki-Lin* behind and slightly above. Matthew admired the independent collectors, who owned their own ships, set their own rates, and worked when they felt like it.

"Goldshield, you're losing altitude," he warned.

"I know. Fuel flow is declining. I don't think I'll make it to Sundown," she said.

"Better tap out your load."

"I can't do that."

"You can't ditch with a billion megawatts in your cells! You'll burn out like a spicule."

"If I'm going to lose my ship, I'll at least need something to salvage," said Gem. They argued briefly, but she wouldn't budge. Without the power, Gem had no margin to absorb the loss of the *Tourmaline*.

Matthew dropped the *Ki-Lin* alongside Gem's ship. He flipped on an exterior viewer. "I can see H-E leaking from a port vent," he said. The short plume of vapor blew back from the *Tourmaline*, dispersing rapidly in the vacuum. "Six hundred fifty kilometers to go. How're you doing?"

"Lovely. Less than two hundred kilos of helium left."

"You'll make it. I can see the shadows from here." Matthew did not exaggerate. From his higher position, the dark band of the Sundown Zone was clearly visible.

"That's it. I'm dry," said Gem. "I'm shutting down now."

"No! Let the pump run till it burns out. You're almost there!"

The *Tourmaline* wobbled and sank toward the surface. Matthew thought for a moment that Gem had lost control, then he saw she was trying to avoid a row of jagged craters ahead. The *Tourmaline* drifted right. A long, shallow-sided ravine appeared.

"Twenty kilometers to go. Stay level," said Matthew. "Give it full thrust. As the pump fails, your power will taper off anyway."

Tourmaline spurted ahead. Gem put the nose down and dived for darkness. Matthew watched, riveted and aghast, as the *Tourmaline* brushed the wall of the ravine. The ship slewed hard to port, dragged a trailing wingtip through the deep dust, and ploughed into the bottom of the ravine. The dipper ship skidded over two thousand meters and came to rest just fifty meters inside the Sundown Zone.

"Jesus H. Christ," said Matthew. "Goldshield! Goldshield, can you hear me?"

"Yeah . . . I'm here," she said slowly.

"Are you hurt?"

"I sorta knocked my head on the console."

"Is it serious?"

"I don't recommend doing this for fun," she said. "Now what happens?"

"I'm staying with you till somebody comes," he said.

"Who'll come? I'm just an independent."

"When word reaches Icecube that you're down, they'll send a pogo to pick you up," he said.

Gem then said what Matthew feared to mention. "If they can find me."

Matthew circled the crash site for twenty minutes. He kept Gem talking to keep her morale up. Talk was good for another reason. Matthew could tell by Gem's growing vagueness that she suffered a concussion.

"'Bout time you left, Lawton," she said. "Fat Yu must be wondering where the hell his ship is by now."

"Fuck Yu," said Matthew. "He's not my mother."

"No jokes, Lawton. Get outta here. You can't do any more. You must be getting low on fuel."

This was true. In another ten minutes, Matthew would not have enough to get back to Icecube. He decided to proceed with an idea he'd been toying with for the past half hour.

"Listen, Goldshield. I'm not leaving you out here to die. I said I'd stay, and I will, even if it means landing beside you."

"Why lose your ship and your job for me? We're not Island-brothers. We've never even met," she said.

"I hope we can someday," he replied. "My rescue beacon's been on since you ditched. When I get down to zero fuel, I'm going to land as close to you as I can. Maybe the Pros in Icecube don't care about an independent, or me, but Yu sure as hell will want *Ki-Lin*'s load. He'll send the pogos for us."

"And kick your ass when he gets here," Gem said.

Ki-Lin's tank went dry fourteen minutes later. Matthew made a horrible mess of a landing, losing all four antennas and burying the forepart of the ship in the deep Mercurian dust. *Ki-Lin* lay less than a hundred meters from the wrecked *Tourmaline*.

"Welcome to Mercury," said Gem.

"Nice to be here in one piece. How're you fixed for oxygen?"

"Ten hours' worth, more or less. My problem is temp," she said. "Everything's fine in the shade, but when the planet rotates me into the sun, I'll cook without helium." Since neither Gem nor Matthew had a pressure suit, they were locked in their ships until found.

"We'll be picked up long before then," said Matthew. Gem muttered something unkind about optimists.

They talked for two solid hours. Gem's attention wandered. To keep her alert, Matthew asked more and more intimate questions.

She said, "I gave up a steady job with Emperor Star Lines to become a dipper. Can you imagine? All I did was usher rich Earthers and Pro aliens around the interiors of plushy passenger ships. 'This is your cabin, sir. The dining room is on the port side, my Pro. Keep your hands to yourself, capper!'"

Matthew laughed. "So you quit to get rich yourself. How long've you been dipping?" he said.

"Two quarters. I had a very short career."

He ignored her gloomy remark. "I've been out here four, ever since I left Luna," he said. "You're a Transaster, aren't you? Which island are you from?" Gem was slow answering. Matthew called sharply, "Gem! Talk to me!"

"I'm tired of talking. Let me rest, will you?"

"No, you might not wake up. Talk to me. Tell me what you look like."

"Huh? Oh, yeah. I'm one hundred and seventy—seventy—" She mumbled a number Matthew couldn't understand. "—centimeters tall. My hair's black . . ."

"Are you married, Gem?"

"Not 'ny more. Divorced."

"Children?"

"Me? Naw. Craig—my ex—had one of those implants Earthers get, that prevents, ahm, fert-fertility."

"You were married to an Earthman? What did he do?"

An audible yawn crossed the com-band. "He was a fact'ry manager for, ahm, Selenica Phar-ma-ceut-tic."

"Yeah? My old man was an engineer. He built a factory on Luna for that company. I remember when we lived in Tycho Basin, he'd come home covered with white mona-tomic dust. Nothing could get that stuff off."

The open band was silent. Matthew called Gem repeatedly, but she didn't answer. He despaired. He had wrecked his ship, endangered his life and his load, all for a woman who was probably dying. Yu would crucify him. He might even prosecute him for damaging the *Ki-Lin*.

Matthew continued to call Gem intermittently. Between calls, he thought feverishly of how he would defend his actions when Yu caught up with him. Perhaps he could plead the Unwritten Law of Space, which held that any ship must go to the aid of another vessel in trouble.

All very noble, and applicable in deep space. The Dippers' Code was the only law near the sun: get thee behind me, competitor.

A new voice crackled through his headmike. "Calling Yu Group ship *Ki-Lin;* this is Icecube Patrol Pogo fifteen. Respond OTB."

"Yes, I hear you. This is Lawton of the *Ki-Lin*. I'm down in the Dante Trough with an independent, Gold-shield of the *Tourmaline*. We're right inside the Sundown Zone," he said.

"Stand by, *Ki-Lin*. We're on our way."

Matthew could not see the pogo, nor hear it land, but he did detect footsteps on the hull when the patrol arrived. They attached a rescue vent to his module and cracked the *Ki-Lin* open.

Two suited figures pulled him from his seat. The one on his left slid her visor back. "Are you intact, Lawton?" she said.

"I'm all right. Let's pick up Gem," he said.

They jumped the pogo from the *Ki-Lin* to the *Tourmaline*. From above, Gem's ship was in much better shape than Matthew's. The pogo touched down softly in the dust millimeters from *Tourmaline*'s port wing.

Though he didn't have a spacesuit, Matthew rushed into the rescue tunnel as soon as it was sealed to Gem's ship. He ripped the release bar free, and the hatch fell down.

Gem was sitting upright, eyes closed. Matthew reached in and touched two fingers to her throat. Her skin was warm, and her pulse beat strongly.

"Gem," he said, patting her face. "Wake up."

Her black Transaster eyes opened. "Who're you?" she said sleepily.

"Matthew Lawton."

"Oh."

Matthew and the pogo crew carried Gem back to the rescue vehicle. He held her head in his lap, and gently pressed a cold compress to the bruise on her forehead.

"What're you staring at?" she said.

"You're very beautiful," said Matthew.

Gem smiled. "Do you always wreck your ship to meet a woman?"

"No, but if this is the result, I may try it more often," he said.

Gem closed her eyes again and slept peacefully in Matthew's arms.

CHAPTER 5

Sian stayed three days. As the last day wound down, Matthew was relieved to see her go. The pleasure he'd felt on her arrival had evaporated. He was bored by her endless talk about the Beneficial Party and what she was going to do in it.

"Enough good people together can change things," she said repeatedly. Matthew refrained from comment. Good people didn't join the BP. Ambitious people did.

They made love only twice. The second time was a disaster. Matthew had not failed so miserably since his early days at school. He knew why; the nightmare was still with him.

Sian decided to leave early. Matthew carried her luggage to the roof. She slid back the skimmer door and stowed her belongings behind the seat.

"Matt," she said, "you've got to do something."

"About what?"

"Your job. You can't keep dipping. You'll kill yourself."

34

"It's all I know," he said. A chill wind washed over them. Matthew thrust his hands in his pockets.

"You have plenty of money. You can live on what you have now for the rest of your life," said Sian.

"And do nothing? How long would I last as one of the idle rich?"

"There are many things on Earth you could involve yourself in," she said.

"Like politics?"

Her expression grew grim. "I used to be able to talk to you," said Sian. "But every time you come back from space you're more distant, more morose." Her voice tightened. "I love you, Matt, but I won't suffer for you because your ego won't let you quit."

He looked away. Sian wedged herself in the pilot's seat. The skimmer's generator began to whine.

"That's all it is!" she shouted. "Ego. Blind, tight-ass male ego!"

The suspension of the skimmer swirled around him. He stood, feet spread apart like a sailor on a heaving deck. Sian punched forward thrust and left him behind. She climbed a hundred meters, banked, and whizzed over Matthew's house. The morning sun glinted on the skimmer's belly as it disappeared east.

Matthew walked to the edge of the roof. From there to the ground was a twenty-meter drop. The mountainside below was all rough stone and tangled vines. A fall from the roof would certainly be fatal.

How's your nerve, Lawton?

He brought his heels together and balanced on the rim of death. Twenty meters was nothing to a dipper.

What're you afraid of? You're the man who robs the sun. The old man of the game. Younger, smarter men and women die in your place. That's why they fear you. They're afraid of your skill. What bargain did you make that keeps you alive?

Oh, Gem, why did you go? Where did you go? Are you there in the sun, somewhere, waiting for me?

Falldon'tfall . . .

Matthew swayed back from the edge. Something was moving below. He bent down on his knees, then his stomach, as he recognized his reclusive neighbor picking her way over the stones.

This was his closest view yet of S. Mackensen. She was rather short, 170 cm or so, and her brown hair was unfashionably long. She walked hesitantly, arms crossed below her breasts, feeling her way among the rocks with her toes. After slipping once or twice, she finally reached the big boulder between her house and Matthew's. She climbed on the boulder, removed her shoes, and draped herself across the stone.

Matthew was fascinated. He descended through the house to the kitchen. A door in the kitchen led to a metal ladder going down to the ground. He lowered himself out the door and circled around the house.

The slope was steep, and Matthew was hard put to keep his balance. As he emerged below his deck, he slipped on some loose rocks. The woman on the boulder opened her eyes and sat up.

"Why are you spying on me?" she said.

"I'm not; I'm just out for a walk," he replied. He took a step closer and the woman gathered herself to flee.

"Wait," said Matthew. "Don't go. I want to talk to you."

She paused, tense, ready to run. Matthew felt as if he were confronting a wild animal in the forest, one not trusting of man. He stepped over a knot of vines and knelt on one knee.

"Who are you?" he said.

"S. Mackensen."

"What does the *S* stand for?"

She thought a moment and answered, "Sasha."

"Well, Sasha Mackensen, you're a hard woman to meet," he said.

"I meant to be," she said. "What do you want?"

"Nothing but friendly conversation. Is that so much?"

"I-I am not a well person. You should not get too close to me."

"You're healthy enough to climb down here to sun yourself," said Matthew.

"I need the sun."

"Don't we all? Look, I've owned this place several years, but I'm often gone for long periods. I've never had a neighbor, and I kind of like the idea. And sure, your elusiveness made me curious, too."

She smiled. "Men are always curious."

He liked her, largely for her looks alone. Sasha wasn't beautiful—which is not to say she was ugly, either. In an era where men and women of all ages could indulge in products and processes to make themselves look young and attractive, Sasha Mackensen was strikingly plain.

Her eyes were brown, under brows that were heavy and unshaped. Compared to Matthew's caramel tone, she was decidedly pale. Her figure was unimposing, and from the way the flesh hung on her arms, Matthew could tell she was no athlete.

He made a small advance toward her. Sasha slid to her feet. "Please," she said. "It would be a mistake for you to get to know me."

"Why?" he said, narrowing the gap still further. He got within two meters before she bolted. Sasha crossed the uneven ground with noteworthy agility and disappeared behind her house.

A sensible man would have gone home. A sensible man would have respected a neighbor's right to privacy. Matthew set off in pursuit of Sasha.

He found a ladder just like his set in the concrete foundation wall. He scaled the rungs to the lower porch, which ran three quarters around the house. The door to the living room was closed, but the codelock had been forced. More than forced, it had been melted. Matthew slid the plexi panel aside and went in.

The morning sun cast sharply angled beams across the room. Nothing marred their symmetry, as there wasn't a single piece of furniture in the whole place. Finding the layout of the Mackensen house was the same as his, Matthew went through each room on the main floor: kitchen, pantry, bathroom, and study. No furniture in the house. No food in the pantry. No Sasha.

Matthew climbed the spiral stairs to the second floor. At the top of the stairs he noticed the carpet had been stripped from the floor. A patch of bare concrete ran from the stairs to the master bedroom. Filled with curiosity (and a certain amount of righteous indignation), Matthew pushed the bedroom door open.

Sasha huddled in the corner, knees drawn up to her chin. "Go away. Leave me alone," she said with quiet force.

"Who are you? Why are you living in an empty house?" said Matthew.

"It's mine, I leased it. I do not have to tell you my business."

"Maybe you'd prefer to speak to the constabulary," he said. He turned to go.

"If I tell you, will you leave me alone?"

"Depends on what you say."

"Twelve days ago my husband died. He was an important man, and the authorities took special interest in the matter. They concluded I had something to do with his death. I fled before they could arrest me," said Sasha.

"You're hiding out," said Matthew. "Did you kill him?"

"No, it was an accident."

Isn't it always, he thought. "What was your husband's name?"

"David Mackensen."

Matthew frowned. "Why is that name familiar?"

"David was the Atlantic Regional Chairman of the Beneficial Party," said Sasha.

CHAPTER 6

Pro Yu was not pleased with his young pilot. Matthew's assistance to Gem Goldshield, while a humane and courageous act, wasn't standard dipper policy.

"This is a hard place," said Yu. "We do not aid a fallen competitor. We step over them and carry on."

"That's not the way I operate!" Matthew retorted. "I'll help any being in distress I find. Any other action is stupid and wasteful!"

Matthew was fired.

Yu didn't prosecute, as that would mean Concordat involvement, but he put out the word to the other fleet owners that Lawton was not to work again. Bentick and Rainbow acceded to Yu's wishes. The independents, by and large, were supportive. They saw in Matthew's act an attitude toward dipping not based on total mercantile success. The concept of camaraderie appealed, and like most great ideas, it spread quickly.

Matthew sulked in his cabin, as anger made him poor company. He wasn't afraid of Yu's sanctions; he was more concerned about how he could get back into the sun. He'd saved almost enough money for his own ship. Perhaps Jack would lend him the rest.

The privacy bell on his door rang. "Enter," he said. It was Gem.

"We've missed you in the lounge," she said. "All the independents want to buy you drinks."

He couldn't help but gawk. God, she was beautiful. Her satin-black hair was severely cut shorter than Matthew's to fit her heatsuit. The perfect symmetry of her face was highlighted by her eyes, two black jewels of onyx.

"You're staring again," she chided.

"Sorry. I should think you'd be used to it by now."

Gem unfolded a seat from the wall and sat down. "You never get used to being looked at as a *thing*," she said. "Even cutting my hair didn't help. Maybe I should wear a mask—then people would take me seriously."

"Don't do that. It would be a hell of a loss."

She changed the subject. "I hear you lost your job."

"It kind of figured, don't you think, after I deliberately cracked up Yu's ship?"

"Which is why I'm here. Why did you do it? It was enough you escorted me down. The Icecube patrol would have found me sooner or later. So why crash with me?"

Matthew leaned back against the metal bulkhead and looked at the ceiling. "I guess I cared," he said. "If I had ditched, I wouldn't want to sit there, alone, waiting for a rescue that might not come. The deadliest thing on Mercury isn't heat or airlessness. It's the loneliness."

Gem rose and came to him. She put a hand to his cheek and kissed him.

"What was that for?" he asked, confused but grateful.

"Caring," said Gem.

Hours later, Matthew had cause to be more grateful still. Gem's body was a new world to him. He grew quite drunk with her beauty. She was calm and patient with

Matthew, and tolerated his enthusiastic clumsiness and selfishness until he learned better.

They rested. The narrow bunk was not designed for two, but they were so closely intertwined they lay as one.

Matthew broke the spell. "Is this my reward for helping you?" he said.

She sighed at his crudeness. "Is that what it seemed like?"

"I don't know. I can't imagine why you would have me when there are better-looking men available."

"Do faces and bodies matter so much?"

Matthew couldn't answer. Gem put her thumb and forefinger over his eyelids and gently closed them.

"You are too honest to think that way," she said.

"How do you know?"

"Until the pogo picked me up, you never saw me. You're hardly sex starved enough to wreck a valuable ship for an unseen woman; ergo, your concern was for me, not my face."

Matthew felt like an ignorant boy. Gem lifted his chin until his eyes met hers.

"I've long wanted to find a sincere man. I could never be sure of the ones I met face to face. They'd stare at my face and my body and I'd always wonder: do they know who I really am? Do they care?"

"I care," said Matthew.

She drew him nearer. Fingers intertwined as their lips met. Their hips slowly closed together. Gem let her head fall back as she drank the dense air.

"Have you heard what they say about sundippers?" she whispered. His mind was too clouded to reply. "They say dippers have the Gift, a special power they release when they make love."

Matthew knew the stories. On his first furloughs back to Earth, the stories had followed him, and he never suffered from loneliness. Strange women could see his skinburn and faded hair and knew what he was. He turned down a few, but not many. Matthew felt no guilt over these brief liaisons; there was no pretence on either side. With Gem it was different.

The hastening pressure drove them on. They clutched at each other, pushed each other, racing toward the fiery corona in tandem. The stories were true. Matthew did give back a bit of the sun. But Gem was a dipper too, so their gifts were exchanged. They slowed and shared an exquisite fire. Spent, aching with delight, Matthew and Gem slept, consumed and renewed by the heat.

Jack Sangamon returned with his ship packed with power. He was not a high-percentage man like Matthew, so a full load for him was a matter of luck. He docked on the sixth pylon and strode to the lounge for a drink.

He spotted Matthew and Gem at a table. Matthew's civilian clothes surprised him.

"Are we dressing for the bar these days?" he said. Matthew waved for him to sit. He introduced Gem.

"G'day," said Jack. "We've rather met before."

"Oh?" said Matthew.

Gem said, "Jack persuaded Rainbow to release me from my contract with her."

"How'd he do that?"

"In my usual smooth and competent manner," said Jack. "Rainy bet Gem's ship against mine on a hand of double-red. I won."

"I flew the *Tourmaline* while I paid Jack off," Gem said. "Now Matt and I are in similar predicaments." They explained about Gem's crash and Matthew's brash voluntary landing. Jack's lean face split wide in a grin.

"I wish I'd seen Yu's face when he heard what you did," he said. Jack laid his long arms across Matthew and Gem's shoulders. "Not to worry, mates. There's a big change coming, and you'll be in on it, I swear."

Change soon arrived in the form of Concordat Commissioner Miranda Kostas. Pro Kostas had been summoned by the independent collectors to investigate suspected abuses by the fleet owners. She arrived in an armed Service dromon with an escort of marines. A series of hearings were convened in Icecube's lounge, and every working dipper was called upon to testify to various suspicious incidents. Each one took his turn before the formidable Commissioner. Gem and Matthew were questioned at length about Gem's crash.

"Did you inspect your helium tank before leaving your mooring?" Pro Kostas said to Gem.

"Yes, my Pro. It was intact and pressurized," said Gem.

The Commissioner held up a golden memo chip, signifying an official Concordat document. "I have here the sworn statement of a mechanic working on this station. He says he was paid five kilolots to puncture the helium tank on the *Tourmaline*. This was done in order to cause pilot Goldshield's death."

"I don't understand," said Gem. "The tank had no leaks when I left."

"As the guilty man explained it, he bored a small hole in the tank when it was empty. He plugged the hole with ice—water ice. When the tank was filled with supercold liquid helium, of course the ice remained frozen. But under flight stress in the bare sunlight on Mercury's bright side, the ice weakened and gave way."

Matthew couldn't contain himself. "Who paid for it? Who wanted Gem dead?" he shouted. Other dippers echoed his question.

Pro Kostas surveyed the furious dippers with severe composure. She said, "The names of the culprits are known to us, and they will be punished." The shouting subsided to an angry murmur. "Too long you sundippers have worked without adequate supervision. If it were in my power, I would install a marine guard and customs officers. This I cannot do, because the charter for Icecube prohibits close regulation.

"You men and women are doing a dangerous job in a difficult environment. I appreciate that. You don't need the additional hazard of sabotage. When greedy men seek to trade lives for money, the Concordat must intervene. Therefore, I have taken Amram Bentick and Wellington Yu into custody for barratry and conspiracy to commit murder."

The lounge erupted in cheers. With Bentick and Yu gone, half the dippers were free to work as they chose. The independents were no longer a minority. A whole new game was beginning, with more freedom and more profit to go around.

"There now, you see," said Jack, strolling arm in arm with Matthew and Gem, "it was only a matter of time before Yu and Bentick screwed themselves."

"One thing I don't get," said Matthew. "Why did the mechanic volunteer information to the Space Service? He was paid off; why burn his employer?"

Jack drew in breath with a hiss. "He was persuaded, that's all. Me and Vender and Beams pegged the bloke, and had a word in his ear." He chuckled pleasantly at the recollection.

Matthew was once more impressed with Sangamon's savvy. "I hope you never have cause to 'have a word' with me," he said.

"Or me," said Gem. They reached the row of lifts that ran to the cabins above.

"Poker tonight?" said Jack. Matthew glanced at Gem.

"I don't think so," Matthew said. Gem squeezed his hand. The two of them entered an elevator, leaving Jack alone. Sangamon stood in front of the closed lift doors, rocking back and forth on his heels.

* * *

Ten days later Matthew had a new ship. He arranged to buy the *Bedouin*, one of the vessels impounded from Bentick's fleet. The *Bedouin* was the latest model, a gracefully curved disc with five hundred collector plates spread over its ventral surface. Jack Sangamon cosigned Matthew's chip when the latter's credit was approved for the purchase.

"I'll have it paid for in two dips," Matthew boasted.

"Maybe. You'll have to pull at least a ninety percent load both times," said Jack.

"I'll pull a hundred," vowed Matthew.

The old Bentick and Yu fleet ships were bought up fast. All the dippers were independents now, except for four who still flew for Rainbow Harvester. Rumor had it she was retiring soon.

Jack and Matthew watched the commotion in the repair shop as the ships were auctioned. Jack seemed preoccupied. He turned his back on the action and let out a deep breath.

"Matthew, mate, the time has come for you to pay up," he said.

"The *Bedouin* payment isn't due for sixty days."

"I don't mean the *Bedouin*. I mean me. You owe me, remember?" Matthew confessed he did not. "Ten kilolots and a favor. That's what you promised to pay me if I could get you a job sundipping."

"Right. I paid you ten kilolots."

Jack said, "There's a favor you can give me." He lowered his voice. "I want Gem," he said.

"What!"

"Calm down, mate. Just a loan, nothing permanent."

"I can't do that, Jack. Gem's a person; I can't give her to anybody."

Sangamon squinted at Matthew. "You love her, don't you?"

"Yes."

"Does she love you?" he asked. Matthew started to say "Of course!" but realized he really didn't know.

"I'm not the one to ask," he said at last. "Gem's her own woman. Talk to her."

Jack did a strange thing then. He blushed. "If I could do it myself, I wouldn't need the favor," he said.

So Matthew found himself in the weird position of asking his lover if she would consider another man. After he hemmed and hawed his way to the point, Gem astonished him by saying yes.

"You will?" he said.

"Why not? I've thought Jack Sangamon attractive for some time. I think I'll enjoy him," she said.

"What about me?"

"What about you? Did you think our relationship was exclusive? Did you ask and did I agree to that?"

"No, but—"

"You thought it would be so." Gem sighed. "Let me tell you how I feel about us, Matt. You are my best friend, and I trust no one else as I do you. I make love with you because I enjoy it, more so because you respond to *me*, not just to gratify yourself. So why can't we enjoy other people too?"

"I don't want anyone else," Matthew said.

"That's very flattering, but it's not my way. Never again will I be bound by the will of another. Even if I don't take other lovers, I must have the option to do so. Do you understand?"

In fact he did not, but he agreed to her terms. Resistance would have ended everything, and that was the most unbearable thought of all.

Two days later, he returned to the cabin on an errand and found the door locked. He knew what it meant, and he left without making his presence known.

Jack later found Matthew on the observation deck. A pair of Transaster ships were queued up to receive their power shipments.

"A difficult job," said Jack, keeping his eye on the tracery of cables from the dipper ships to the colony vessel. "The slightest mistake and the whole collection goes up like a nova."

Matthew looked at his knuckles, blanched white from gripping the cold metal rail. "I don't know what to say," he said. "I don't know how I should feel about all this."

"Be proud," Jack said. "She speaks mostly of you."

"Straight?"

"Straighto, mate."

The nearer power freighter slipped free of the gossamer lines and fired its maneuvering motor. The nose came about slowly, inexorably, until it pointed away from Icecube toward deep space.

"You can't be angry, Matthew my lad. You mean more to Gem than anyone. As for me, well, I'm just an old man warming my hands at your fire."

Jack held out his hand. Matthew glanced at the open brown palm, then grasped it tightly with both hands.

CHAPTER 7

Matthew kept his audion cooking all night. Since returning from Sasha's, he thought he could get on her good side if he brought her some food. He ordered a week's worth of groceries, and set the audion to making fresh bread, pasta, and reheatable casseroles. It was the neighborly thing to do, and it was a good way to use up his stock of reconstituted meat. Matthew couldn't stomach ersätz flesh.

He teetered across the sloping ground between their houses, his arms full of cartons. In a fit of true generosity, he had included three bottles of precious North Hemi wine. They clinked together ominously as he sought safe footholds among the rocks.

Climbing the ladder to Sasha's porch proved a heroic task. At length he had his burden safely stacked at the top of the ladder. Matthew went to the broken door and knocked loudly.

"Sasha," he called. "It's Matthew. I've got something

for you." She did not appear. He pulled back the door and put his head inside. He was about to shout again when he noticed the strange music.

A man was singing, but it wasn't like any song Matthew had ever heard. It wasn't Skywave, Martian colonial, or Freyan. The sound was odd, too: curiously hollow and remote, like a faraway echo of a song long since finished.

He traced Sasha by the music. She was upstairs in her sad, empty bedroom, listening to this peculiar song:

Till the End of Time
Long as stars are in the blue
Long as there's a spring, a bird to sing, I'll go on
    loving you . . .
So take my heart in sweet surrender
And tenderly say that I'm
The only one you'll love and live for
Till the End of Time.

"Sasha?" he said.

Her head was hanging low. She looked up at Matthew. "Why are you here?" she said.

"I brought you some food." He spotted the source of the music. It was a rectangular box, fifty cm by forty. A flat black disc rotated on this box and a slim metal rod rested on the disc. The sound emanated from the sides of the box.

"What's that thing?" asked Matthew.

"A music player. My husband was an avid collector of antique machines. When I fled, the only thing I could take with me was this device, and a few discs," she said. Matthew picked up one. It was finely grooved, and there was writing in the center inside a smooth paper circle.

"Perry Como. Nat King Cole. Frank Sinatra," Matthew read from different labels.

"David called these 'elpees,'" said Sasha. "He had over thirty of them. Some are broken now."

"You like music? You should hear my musicon. I have a chip of Beethoven's Seventh that'll loosen your hair."

"Why are you here?" she said again. "I asked you not to visit."

"There's food in the kitchen," said Matthew. "I don't know how you've managed to live here without eating."

Sasha gave him a brief but intense glance. "It has been difficult doing without," she said. She took the elpee off the player. "But it would be better for me not to feed."

Matthew shrugged. "I'll stow the goods I brought. When you get hungry, you'll find them," he said. He started for the door, paused, and added, "You didn't answer my question."

"Which question?"

"Do you like music?"

"Music," said Sasha, "is the most valuable thing humanity has created."

He might have argued with her on this point, but she set the metal rod on a new disc and singing filled the barren room:

> Whispers in the dark—
> Not for laughing or having a lark,
> Saying things that always come true,
> Except for me and you.

Matthew put the food away. Upstairs the singing continued. He cast a quick look at the ceiling, then ducked into the audion service closet. A few minutes' tinkering accomplished his purpose. He could now listen and watch any room in Sasha's house that held a terminal.

Sian called.

"I feel really bad about how I left the other day," she said. "It's no fun fighting with you. You're too serious."

"I take no prisoners," agreed Matthew. "Want to make up?"

"Yes, and I want to have a party."

"Party? Where?"

"Your place, of course," said Sian.

His grimace was plain even by telaudion. "Not with the Photech Funsters," he said. "All they're interested in is free alcohol, drugs, and a chance to get laid."

"Oh? And what are *your* intellectual pursuits?"

"I lost all interest in intellect after I met you," he said.

"Ha, ha. Are we fighting again?"

"No. When do you want this party?"

"The fifty-seventh?" Three days hence. Matthew would have to order extra food, drink, and sociables from his warehouse in Lenoir. "Is that enough time for you?" said Sian.

"I guess so. Can I invite someone I know?"

"Matt, it's your house, remember?"

"Good of you to remind me. I finally met my neighbor, and I think it'd be good for her to mix with people," he said.

"Her? Who is she?" said Sian.

"Her name's Sasha," he said. He couldn't bring himself to mention her last name. Sian probably knew David Mackensen.

"Attractive?"

"Yes." A witty remark begged for release, but for some reason Matthew suppressed it. It was then he realized how much he was attracted to Sasha.

"You're being very tight lipped, Mr. Lawton. I think I'll come down before the party to make sure you're behaving yourself," said Sian.

"Be sure to knock before entering."

Sian compressed her lips and glared. "Bastard! What am I going to do with you?" she said.

He smiled wickedly. "Remember Kerr Lake? The boathouse?"

Sian blushed vividly. "All right," she said. "I'll see you on the fifty-sixth."

" 'Bye, Shy."

"I love you, Matt." There was an awkward silence. He finally nodded curtly before Sian's image faded from the cube.

Matthew broke down the components of his musicon into four manageable loads. The two lighter ones he stuck to pads on his back and carried the others in his hands. His pockets jingled with music chips, ranging from the Magnetic Monopoles (Number One Skywave artists) to Prokofiev's Sixth Symphony. Surely some of this mix would appeal to Sasha.

Her house smelled bad. Matthew found the reason for the stench in the kitchen. A package of freeze-dried chicken was lying thawed and swollen on the counter. A portion of the raw meat looked as if it had been chewed.

Disgusted, Matthew dumped the rotted meat into the disposer. The fetid mass dissolved and vanished. He tapped a panel on the wall and flushed the house with cool, fresh air.

"Sasha? Sasha! It's me, Matthew!" he called. He tried the bedroom, but she wasn't there. Sasha was nowhere upstairs. He checked downstairs and finally found her huddled in the power service closet, where the laser cables were housed. She had scraped the protective coating from a Clearfibre cable and was picking the line itself with her nails.

"Stop that! You want to kill yourself?" Matthew snapped. He pulled her hands away from the cable.

"No, I need it! I starve!" she said plaintively.

"Are you crazy? That's coherent light. It'll burn you," he said. Sasha slumped against his legs.

"Come on, I'll fix you something to eat," he said. He

was beginning to think Sasha was mentally ill. First trying to eat raw chicken, then laser beams! The woman had a definite problem.

Matthew hauled Sasha to her feet. Her arms felt surprisingly firm. She smelled clean, but was innocent of any cosmetic drug or process. He stifled an urge to kiss her.

He left her leaning against the wall in the kitchen while he placed a shrimp casserole in the microwave. He pierced the top of one of his wine bottles and poured two drinks into the cheap plexi cups he'd provided.

"Bon chance," he said, touching his cup to hers.

"You must go away," she said very faintly. "Not to your house. Far away."

"Why? Is being near you going to kill me?"

Sasha dropped her full cup on the floor. "It may," she said.

"I'm not afraid of the Beneficial Party. I've got money; I can buy as many constables as they send at me. And if they try to get rough, well, I know a thing or two about killing, too."

He assembled the musicon on the kitchen floor. As he clipped the various parts together, he explained how they worked. Sasha watched listlessly.

"What would you like to hear? Popular? Classical?" he said.

"No difference."

He chose Prokofiev. The First Violin Concerto suited his mood very well. It was a poignant, airy work, from the composer's early period. The soloist, Ngo Van Thuy, was a master.

Sasha did perk up as the concerto got under way. "Is there singing?" she asked.

"No, strictly instrumental," said Matthew. She listened intently. "Like it?" he said.

"Not as well as Perry Como."

The rippling second movement was half gone when the first flicker of lightning revealed itself in the southeast. Thunderheads loomed over Salt Rock Gap. Sasha stiffened as thunder rolled over the Black Mountains.

"What's the matter?" said Matthew.

"Is it an electrical storm?" she said.

"Yeah, we have them all the time. There's no danger. These houses are well grounded."

"Lightning is very hazardous!"

"We're safe inside," Matthew insisted.

The flashes crept closer. With each bolt Sasha grew more and more agitated. When the first stroke burst through the clouds in full view, she cried out in pain and collapsed.

Matthew examined her carefully. Her eyes stared widely. Thunder boomed into the house, drowning Ngo Van Thuy in its mighty peals.

Sasha twitched violently every time lightning broke forth. Her muscles surged as if the crude electricity were passing through them.

"What can I do?" said Matthew helplessly.

"Too much," said Sasha. Her hand moved convulsively and grabbed his arm. "Stay—till storm—is over," she said.

The concerto ended, but the concert of nature continued. The clouds blackened and a torrent of rain fell. A large brown and gray bird, confused by the storm, crashed against the plexi windows. It spread its wings and flew at the invisible obstacle again and again, until it battered itself to death. The wind and the rain carried the body over the edge of the porch, leaving only a few broken feathers imbedded in the vinyl seal under the window.

The storm hastened on. By 15:00, the rain had stopped. Matthew removed the cold casserole from the oven and threw it, tray and all, over the porch rail.

He didn't know what to do for Sasha. She was almost

tetanic. He flexed her arms and wrists, so she wouldn't stiffen up further. Gradually she lost this unnatural rigidity.

Matthew stayed several hours past sunset. He put a Chopin chip on. A piece played that sounded familiar. He discovered that Sasha's favorite song ("Till the End of Time") was based on Chopin's Polonaise in A-flat.

The music stirred Sasha. She sat up. "It was kind of you to stay," she said.

"But now I have to go, is that it?"

"Yes, Matthew."

"Right."

He went down on one knee as if to retrieve his music chips. Instead, he closed Sasha in his arms and kissed her.

She neither resisted nor cooperated. Matthew had the distinct impression she didn't know how to respond. He held the kiss, hoping to provoke some sort of reaction. He did.

Sasha raised her right hand and placed a thumb and two fingers on Matthew's chest, over his heart.

He flinched. A fiery sensation flowed through his chest from his heart to his brain. It burst there and he nearly passed out. Sasha gasped and snatched her hand away. Matthew fell back and sat down hard.

"Jesus!" he said.

His vision slowly cleared. The white stars faded and his ears ceased ringing. Matthew looked at Sasha. His romantic notions were gone, replaced by an inexplicable fear.

CHAPTER 8

Sundippers measure their lives not in days, quarters, or years, nor by the number of dips made, but rather by the amount of power they have collected. One will say, "I'm a five hundred bmW," or "I'm working on my second hundred." A hundred billion megawatts is the standard by which dippers mark their lives.

Jack Sangamon reached the lofty plateau of nine hundred billion megawatts on the eighty-third day of the second quarter, Concordat Year 132. This made him the third-highest ranking dipper of all. Ahead of him were Rainbow Harvester (1,100 bmW), who was living but inactive, and the godlike Dunphy, who had perished after collecting 1,470 bmW.

They held a floating celebration for Jack. Dippers and Icecube personnel drifted in and out, drinking and popping Sting pods under their noses. Matthew returned from his eleventh dip to find the party at one of its high points, with Gem and Jack dancing around the lounge as a musicon played "Eljen à Magyar."

Someone thrust a tall glass of *E*-vodka into Matthew's hand. As his two friends stumbled to a stop, laughing and panting, he called for attention.

"Ladies and gentlemen; I give you Jack 'the Ripper' Sangamon, the greatest active sundipper!" declared Matthew. The lounge floor rattled with shouts of approval. Jack bowed theatrically.

"To the greatest dipper ever!" cried Gem. The crowd was so well lubricated they cheered this exaggeration lustily.

The cheering faded abruptly. Matthew turned to see why. Across the lounge came a lone figure swathed in a loose robe.

"Rainbow," said Gem.

The robed and hooded woman approached the glowing Sangamon. He waited respectfully for her to reach him.

Rainbow offered Jack a hand so thin and delicate it scarcely belonged on a living being. He clasped it gently. Like fine porcelain, it might shatter if held too roughly.

Matthew couldn't see Pro Harvester's face, but he heard her light, indistinct voice conversing with Jack. Sangamon's eyes were attentive as he listened, and he nodded repeatedly.

Rainbow turned away and walked slowly back to the elevators. The assembled men and women of Icecube stood in silent tribute as she passed.

"Amazing," said Matthew.

"Why doesn't she go home? She's so frail," said a young dipper, a muscular fellow named Mitchell Vine.

Gem glared. "This is her home," she said. "Rainbow's been here more than twenty-nine quarters."

Jack joined them. He seemed disturbed.

"What did she say?" asked Matthew.

"She congratulated me. Then she told me to quit as soon as I could."

"Why?" said Gem.

"She said the odds were getting too high against me. Any day I might succumb while dipping—or worse."

Vine said, "What could be worse than a dipping accident?"

"Cancer," said Jack. "Rainbow has four kinds, and they're eating her alive."

Nothing more was said about Rainbow or retirement around Jack. The day after the party he was his crafty self again. He busied himself in the shop, trying to get *Red Jack* ready for his next dip. Matthew and Gem spent the same day together, catching up on the time they'd missed when both were out working.

They left their cabin long enough for dinner. They behaved like happy children, hips bumping as they walked, laughing over the most trivial things. Matthew made a perfect fool of himself with his lo mein noodles, and Gem nearly choked with mirth.

Jack walked in, clad in his all-white heatsuit. Only the dark oval of his face showed, and the bones beneath the tight white mesh worked like the forbidden mechanism of an android.

"G'day," he said. "We who are about to fry salute you." It was a tired old quip, but Jack always said it before leaving. He was terribly superstitious.

"Have a drink before you go," said Matthew. "A little liquid courage never hurts."

"No thanks," said Jack rather flatly.

"Have a noodle then," said Gem, holding out a finger with a few centimeters of brown pasta dangling from it. She and Matthew giggled between their teeth.

"You two have the sillies," said Jack. "I can see there's no point hanging around here. I'll see you in twelve hours."

"Not me," said Gem. "I'm out at sixteen-thirty my-self."

"Oh? Trying to give me a little competition?"

"We have to keep the old man on his toes," said Matthew. If Jack had one sensitive spot, it was his age. He bristled at Matthew's remark.

"Balls to you, boy. Would you care to bet who brings back a bigger load?" he said.

"I have eight kilolots that say you don't get sixty-five percent this dip," said Gem.

"Ha, ha! Little girl, I haven't pulled less than eighty since I was Lawton's age," said Jack.

"How long ago was that, Jack?" said Matthew, grin-ning. "Twenty years?"

Jack ignored this jab and faced Gem. "Make it twenty K and you're on," he said. She agreed.

Twenty thousand was a ridiculous sum for two people to wager when their estimated take from a decent dip was four to six million. It was strictly a matter of competitive pride. Neither Jack nor Gem wanted to lose a single millilot to the other.

The lounge PA announced, "Attention, John San-gamon. Stand to your ship. Fire Lane opens in twenty minutes."

Gem and Matthew stood. Jack put one arm around Gem's waist and kissed her deeply. Matthew looked at his shoes. When Sangamon offered him his hand, Matthew regarded it warily. Their palms touched, then Jack yanked Matthew forward and threw his arms around the younger man and hugged him ferociously.

"Well! I see who you're going to miss most," said Gem. Jack winked. "It's his brown eyes," he said.

"Get out, old flaker," said Matthew, knotting a fist. "Go on, or they'll close the Lane on you."

"Will you be here when I get back?"

"Yeah, I can't leave till they finish repacking the cells on the *Bedouin*," said Matthew.

"Good. We'll get blitzed on the money Gem's going to owe me," said Jack. The PA called for Sangamon again. "'Round we go!" he said, trotting away.

"Banzai!" called Gem to his back.

They went to the viewports to watch Sangamon leave. He had only fifteen minutes to get his ship to the bright side of Mercury. The Fire Lane could only be opened at distinct intervals, as its power supply had to build up over a long period of time. Old-time dippers used to take their chances in the corona's two-million-degree heat. Modern pilots preferred the Fire Lane. Any edge was welcome.

Jack rolled the stingray-shaped *Red Jack* wing-over-wing as he pulled away from Icecube. He was showing off more than usual. Had Matthew reflected, he might have thought of Rainbow's warning and not chided Jack about his age.

Red Jack emerged from Mercury's penumbra and blazed like a new star. Even far distant, the sundipper burned with the sun's reflected fury. The sparkling ship disappeared around the dark bulk of Mercury.

The time came for Gem to leave. Matthew wrapped the zipseams of her heatsuit together, making sure there were no gaps. She turned to face him, and he noticed for the first time how dark her skin was getting. The white synthetic mesh really set it off.

"What's the matter?" she said.

"Nothing. The trade's beginning to show on you," he replied.

Gem looked past Matthew to a mirror. "Not bad," she said. "Do you think I'll end up looking like Jack?"

"God, I hope not!" Gem smiled and kissed him on the nose.

Matthew couldn't go to the launch room at the end of

the pylon where Gem's ship, *Topaz,* was moored. He stayed in the workshop observatory overlooking the pylon as Gem prepared to depart.

She slipped into the cupola of the *Topaz.* Before the lid was snugged, she looked up at the workshop window. He couldn't hear her through the thick plexi, but her mouth formed the word *banzai.*

May you live ten thousand years.

The *Topaz* slipped free of the space station and flew out on an opposite heading from the *Red Jack.* Gem always made her dips retrograde to Mercury's orbit. Many dippers believed retrograde was safer, as it insured Icecube would be coming toward the returning ship. The elegant discoidal *Topaz* was soon swallowed by darkness, with only its blinking navigation lights revealing its diminishing position.

Matthew went to the *Bedouin*'s berth. He had a contract with Island Epsilon to deliver eighty billion megawatts by the end of the quarter. Few dippers would bind themselves to an explicit contract, preferring as they did to deal on a per-dip basis. Matthew was good enough to deliver what he promised. He liked the pressure to perform, and he expected the maintenance team on Icecube not to let him down.

The crew overhauling the *Bedouin* argued and bickered with Matthew and each other over the proper installation of the new storage cells. He was at the point of shaking a plasma torch under Chief Mechanic Arne Dawlish's nose when the station-wide PA system interrupted.

"Attention, all personnel! This is a station alert. Smoker coming in. Repeat, smoker coming in!" it blared.

All free hands rushed to the lounge. Everyone crowded to the viewports and watched, wondering what friend of theirs was in trouble.

"There!" cried a woman at the east panel. Sure enough, a ship was approaching on a tangential course, burning as it came. Vapor trailed behind it, giving it the appearance of a miniature comet.

"Can you tell who it is?" said Matthew to Mitchell Vine, who was in front of him.

"I think it's the Dog," said Vine. Ian "the Dog" McLane was a Martian colonial. His ship, *Rover Boy,* was marked with a red hound's head silhouette.

The Dog it was, coming in fast for the fourth pylon. Matthew clenched his teeth as *Rover Boy* bored in. *Bedouin* was moored on the fifth pylon, and if McLane lost control, he might hit Matthew's ship.

Rover Boy skewed wildly, braking thrusters flaring. The woman on Matthew's right screamed. Arne Dawlish shouted, "He's going to hit!"

Icecube shuddered slightly as the Dog piled his ship into the fourth pylon. The bare metal girders ripped through the shiny skin of *Rover Boy.* Matthew threw an arm over his eyes and waited for the pent-up sunpower to flash them all out of existence.

Nothing happened. "Must've tapped out his cells," said Arne.

Without any urging, the assembled dippers made for the scene of the crash. By the time Matthew got there, McLane had been pulled free of his cupola and was lying on the shop floor. His heatsuit was scorched brown. His faceshield came away with most of McLane's skin on it. Somebody shouted for the medics.

Len Rackham, Icecube's manager, knelt by McLane. "Ian, what'd they do to you?" he said.

"Goddamn solar flare," said McLane. "I musta passed within a thousand km of it." A medic arrived. She pumped Steral into his neck to ease his burns, and set up a skin pack filled with Crux to deaden the pain.

McLane's skinless lips moved slowly. "Has the other one come in?" he said.

"Other?" said Rackham. "You're the only smoker we've had."

McLane coughed. "I-I detected another ship on a parabolic course," he said. "When the flare went up, I saw him dive."

"Down? Didn't he flake?" said Rackham.

"Uh-uh. My motion sensor had him diving before it overloaded and blew."

Rackham turned to Arne and said, "It could've been a shadow effect, or a packet of plasma, but we have to check. Have the flight center project all the parabolics of the past ten hours back to us. See if it can tell who the other dipper might've been."

The Crux got to McLane. As his body went limp, the medics heaved him onto a carry-pad for the clinic. Three hours later he would be dead.

Matthew picked up McLane's faceplate. The plexi fibers were fused into a hard, brittle shell. As he gazed at the contorted mask, a thin rivulet of blood ran off the inner surface and trickled down his hand.

Arne Dawlish came back. His expression was grim. "Track analysis says the diver was *Red Jack*," he said slowly.

"It couldn't be!" Matthew exploded. Jack knew better than to try and dive under a solar flare.

"Eighty-five percent probability," said Arne.

This rose to 100 percent when Jack never returned.

Matthew was numb with disbelief. He went to the lounge and awaited Gem's arrival. He drank until he was stiff with anger. Why Jack? Why him?

Dippers offered sympathy. He damned them as hypocrites. Every time a dipper died, the privileges enjoyed by the dead pilot were reapportioned among the living. The prevailing rates on harvested power also went up. Everyone, including Matthew and Gem, would profit from Jack's death.

Matthew vomited a bellyful of liquor in his cabin toilet and prepared to leave without waiting for Gem. He flew the *Bedouin* out to expend his anger and anguish in space.

He raced through the photosphere with Tchaikovsky's Sixth Symphony. Never had he flown so fast, so skillfully. The sun can be beaten, thought Matthew; I can steal your power and you can't hurt me.

He soaked up ninty-seven percent of capacity in one plunge. Not good enough! Though low on fuel and coolant, he dipped again to top off his cells. One hundred percent. Nothing less would ever do again.

The transport *Menzel* arrived at Icecube to receive Matthew's harvest. The *Bedouin* was wedded to the transport by a thousand fine cables. Transferring energy took five times as long as gathering it, because no cable made could safely carry the power of one dipper cell.

While the transfer continued, Matthew shared a drink with Card Traphand, the *Menzel*'s Energy Agent.

"This load will provide us with power for two quarters," said Traphand. "Island Epsilon is grateful for your speed and efficiency."

Matthew tossed back fifty cc's of *E*-vodka and said, "I'm grateful for the money."

"Of course. Here you are." The agent handed Matthew a memo chip that credited the Earthman's account with nine point fifty-seven megalots. "Would you like the payment confirmed?" he said.

"Not necessary," said Matthew. Any colony that stiffed a dipper wouldn't be able to buy a candle until accounts were settled to the dipper's complete satisfaction.

"When can we expect the next delivery?" said Traphand.

"Not for a while. I'm taking a holiday."

The agent frowned. "Are you not well? Was the payment insufficient?"

"I need rest," said Matthew. "I'm losing my perspective, so I'm taking some time off, spend some of the money I've earned while I can."

"A wise idea. Only I hope you will return to us, Mr. Lawton. You have an admirable record. We prefer to deal with you over any others. Sundippers come and go, but yours is a rare skill," said Traphand.

Matthew held out his cup for a refill. A slight tremor passed down his arm.

"Skill, my Pro, is no longer enough," he said.

Gem got the bad news when she moored. Her reaction to Jack's death was cooler and more philosophical than Matthew's.

"It's the hazard we all face," she said. "My own family gave me up for dead when they learned I was becoming a dipper."

"Doesn't it bother you at all that Jack's dead?" he said.

"Yes, Matt. He was a good friend, a great dipper, and a considerate lover. I shall miss him. But there's much power to collect, and there're fewer of us now to gather it. I shall work hard and remember Jack. What else can I do?"

"You could visit Earth with me," he said. "I'm buying a house in West Hemi. I could use your input. I-I don't want to go there alone."

"Ground life isn't for me. I was born in space, and I'll always live in space." She shivered slightly. "The idea of being at the bottom of all that atmosphere repels me," she said.

Gem held to her resolution even as she walked Matthew to meet his Earth-bound transport. The Martian vessel *Thorpe* was moored where the *Red Jack* had last berthed.

After a quiet embrace, Matthew said very solemnly, "I love you, Gem."

"It is good to be loved," she replied.

The boarding tunnel hissed shut. Gem did not stay by the viewport to see Matthew go.

CHAPTER 9

Matthew fled from Sasha so hastily after the thunderstorm he left his treasured musicon behind. He stumbled back to his house through the wet vines and slippery rocks. He went directly to the revival room. The diagnostic function of the house audion scanned him for injuries.

"Aside from an accelerated heartbeat and blood pressure, I find you quite normal, sir," said the audion. Matthew popped a tranquilizer pod under his nose anyway.

Standing in the bathroom under the water jet, he examined his chest. There were three whitish spots, points on an equilateral triangle, above and to the right of his left nipple.

Something *did* happen. Matthew could not explain what Sasha had done, but it both frightened and intrigued him.

A football broadcast from Luna held his interest only briefly. Without music he grew bored. The audion refused to sing. Entertainment, it said tartly, was not one of its functions.

Inevitably he went outside to look at Sasha's house. Luna was waxing full. Her bright light silvered South Fork Creek in the distance and made the stark white pillars of the upper house stand out like bleached bones.

A chill unrelated to the weather gripped Matthew. He shook it off and went to bed.

The house wakened him. It was late, past 10:30. "The comestibles you ordered from Lenoir have arrived, sir," it said.

Matthew raised his head from the pillow. The room was a blur. "The what?" he mumbled.

"Food and supplies for the party, sir. Shall I have the handlers leave the goods on my roof?"

"Sure, sure."

Matthew rose feeling weak and empty. He attributed this to a lack of dinner and too much reliance on drugs. He cooked his own breakfast while the audion saw to the party supplies.

Two eggs and a quarter kilo of sausage later, Matthew felt much strengthened. He decided to retrieve his musicon from Sasha. Before going, he tuned his telaudion to pick up any sounds within her house. He heard nothing, not even breathing.

Reversing the signal, he called her. Sasha answered, and when she knew it was Matthew, allowed the holoid cube to display her image as well.

"I went in such a hurry last evening I forgot my musicon," he said.

"Yes, you did," said Sasha.

"I'd like to have it back. May I come and get it?"

"It is where you left it."

"I need it for the party I'm having day after tomorrow," said Matthew. "I was wondering if you'd care to come."

"No, Matthew. I do not want to be around people."

"You should come. The guests'll all be friends of Sian's, from the Triangle. They won't know you. Hell, they don't know me."

Sasha looked thoughtful. "Sian is your lover?" she asked.

"Uh, yes."

"Will her friends include men and women?"

"Yeah. Shy works hard to get a fifty-fifty mix. She says it makes for a livelier group if the possibility of sex exists equally for all," he said. Suddenly Matthew was embarrassed. By Sian's own dictum, Sasha would be the odd-woman out.

"I will come, Matthew, but you must not tell anyone who I am or why I am there. And ask no questions if I leave in someone's company," she said.

Why not mine? he thought. No, Sian would be there.

"You're an adult," he said blithely. "Do what you want."

He went over after noon to fetch his musicon. For the first time, Sasha greeted him at the door. She was wearing that blue kimono again and was barefoot.

Matthew gathered his music chips. He broke the player into components for easier carrying. Sasha watched him work.

"You are concerned about me," she said.

"I don't know who you are," he replied without looking up.

"It is too late to pretend we are ordinary people," said Sasha. "So I will tell you I am as frightened of you as you are of me."

He started to snap "Who's afraid?" but didn't. She wouldn't be fooled by bravado.

Matthew stuck the musicon components on his back and got to his feet. Sasha seemed taller than before. He realized this was the first time they had faced each other standing.

"Want to see the marks?" he said in a low voice.

She shook her head and held out her hand. The tips of the three fingers she'd touched him with were blistered.

"I have my own."

Sian descended on Buncombe Horse Range Ridge like a thunderbolt. She was bursting with enthusiasm for the party, as most of her Triangle friends had never met the marvelous Matthew. In spite of his contempt for the Photech Funsters, Matthew caught her excitement and willingly worked with her on setting out the food and sociables. The audion asked what to do if a guest requested an unfamiliar mixed drink.

"Before twenty-two hundred, give them vodka. After twenty-two, give them white table wine," said Sian. "Sober, they'll be too polite to complain. Drunk, they'll drink wine and like it."

"Ah, logic," said Matthew.

He spent half the afternoon bolting sections to the deck railing to raise them. It would be bad form to lose guests over the side. As he worked, Sian brought him a glass of fresh orange juice.

"Tell me about this mysterious neighbor of yours," she said.

"Not so mysterious. She's recently widowed, and very shy."

"What's her name again?"

He squirted jelsteel into a rivet hole. "Sasha," he said.

"I mean her last name, dummy."

"She didn't say."

Sian cocked an eyebrow. "She didn't give you a last name, and you invited her to our party? Must be gorgeous."

"Not at all. Hand me the glue, will you?"

Sian slapped the tube on his palm. "Well, I want to meet her. The last 'friend' you made on Earth was me, and look what happened to us!" she said.

CHAPTER 10

Life in Icecube was different after Jack's death. The gambling, the money-making, the jollity went on, but it seemed two-dimensional without Sangamon's enormous zest for life.

Gem was good for Matthew in this period. What he once damned as her coldness, he learned to appreciate as wisdom. They stayed together nearly all the time, though their lovemaking was less frequent. It seemed less important now; having someone to touch and confide in was more so.

Days dropped into the past and vanished like escaping solar flares. Gem's black hair developed strands of white. Matthew's had long since become colorless. The sun etched his face with strong lines, and his skin took on the permanent tone of rubbed teak.

During the low point of the eleven-year sunspot cycle, every dipper was busy plunging in the sun, trying to make some extra money in the "safe" period. Matthew stuck to his own schedule. Two quarters on, two off. Dip less and live longer. He had learned that from Jack.

Icecube was nearly empty when he met Rainbow Harvester. Everyone was out save the sick and the injured. Matthew descended to the lounge, expecting to find it vacant. Instead he saw a solitary hooded figure at a table in the center of the room.

He was amazed. Though no word had circulated, he'd assumed Rainbow had died long ago. With four kinds of cancer, she was nearer to death than life.

He approached her slowly. "Pro Harvester, may I join you?" he said. An emaciated hand lifted from the table and beckoned him to sit.

"I'm surprised to see you here," said Matthew.

"Every day is a surprise," said Rainbow. Her voice was clear but distant. "Are you ill, Mr. Lawton? Is that why you're not working?"

"It's not my time to work," he said. "I have twenty-six more days of rest."

"Ration your time well. It cannot be renewed."

Matthew ordered coffee. He saw Rainbow was having apple juice, so he bought her another glass. She inserted a long, thin tube into the glass and sucked the pale amber juice noiselessly into her hood.

"Has it always been like this when the sunspots diminish?" asked Matthew.

"What a genteel inquiry about my age. How many cycles do you think I've seen?" she said.

"I beg your pardon. I meant no disrespect—"

"No matter, Mr. Lawton. I cannot be offended. Long ago I lost my vanity. One does not keep a mirror on hand to watch the progress of skin cancer."

A feeling of deep sadness touched Matthew. He wanted to comfort her in some way. All he could offer was conversation.

"Tell me about yourself," he said suddenly. "Ever since

I could remember, I've heard stories about you. One reason I became a dipper was because of the fantastic tales told about you and the other greats."

Fingers as slender as death crossed the table and rested weightlessly on his arm. "What have you heard about me?" said Rainbow.

"I'd hate to say, if they weren't true."

"A story for a story, Mr. Lawton. Please."

Matthew said, "Just fragments, really; the 'have you heard' kind of rumor that expands as it's told to more and more people. Such as, I heard you spacewalked the corona in an ordinary Skyweb suit."

"I did."

"How could you've survived? What about the heat? The radiation?"

"You share the common misconception that because the incandescence of the corona is measured at two million degrees Kelvin, it must be hot," said Rainbow. "In truth, it is so rarified as to be nonexistent, heat-wise."

"But the radiation—"

"Is real and quite deadly," she said. "As my current condition proves."

Her glass went dry. The tube vanished into the robe, and for a second Matthew caught a glimpse of Rainbow Harvester's throat. It resembled in color and texture a ring of rotted black leather.

"Did you actually spend twenty-four hours in the photosphere searching for Reggie Momar when he was lost?" asked Matthew.

"It was twenty-one hours, not twenty-four."

"How could you stand it? How could your ship stand it? You didn't have electrostatic dissipators in those days."

"The human body and its extension, the machine, can bear far more than most people imagine," she said.

On they went, Matthew dredging up every wild story of his youth, and Rainbow confirming, denying, or chuckling at them. She grew serious again when Matthew said, "Who was the love of your life? Was it Dunphy? Or Momar?"

"If you mean a man, the one I cared for above all others was the same one who drove me to the sun. He was an Earthman, like you. His name was Philip Bowen. He was nobody, but when he left me for another woman, I was so hurt I decided to end my life in spectacular fashion, by throwing myself into the sun."

"Seems like an elaborate way to kill yourself," he said.

"I always was a dramatic person," said Rainbow. "Obviously, I never went through with my plan. The sun burned away my hatred, and kept me alive all these quarters."

"Only to kill you slowly with cancer."

"The sun didn't cause my illnesses," said Rainbow. "They came from extraneous radiation. The core of the sun is pure and clean. You know it pulses? It is a great fiery heart, pumping life-giving heat and light to the planets. Never hate the sun, Mr. Lawton. You might as well hate God."

He had no answer for this. Sometimes he did hate God.

"The sun bleeds its life away for us. It moans. Have you ever heard it? Don't think me demented, it's true. Next time you dip, tune your com-band between the twelfth and thirteenth bands. Where void should be, you'll hear the sun moan," she said.

"Must be a natural phenomenon," said Matthew.

"Pain is natural, Mr. Lawton. The sun never rests. It burns and burns, every second of every hour for eleven billion years. It made us and all our kind. The energy it emits is life itself. How do you suppose the rumors of sexual prowess among dippers began?"

"I assumed male dippers created the myth to make getting laid easier," he said.

"Reasonable. But think, Mr. Lawton; would such

stories persist if there was no objective reality behind them?" said Rainbow. "Haven't you felt the Gift yourself, with Gem?"

Ideas coalesced in his mind. "Yes," he said. "I always thought it was her doing." He flushed slightly. "That, or love."

"Much of it is. I know her. She worked for me, and I loved her. Anyone who comes close to Gem will love her. She has received the sun's gift, too. We all have, all who have felt its golden breath."

Matthew said, "You speak of sundipping as an almost magical process."

Rainbow folded her hands into her deep sleeves. "It is. We take away crude energy to power our machines. The sun, in turn, shares its life-power with us. Our bodies are the collectors, and we give it to those who share our flesh. That's the secret, Mr. Lawton. That's why I'm still alive."

"Do the others know? Does Gem?"

"They will not believe you if you tell them. Most are here to make money. Life, freedom, and love would not keep them at Icecube for a millisecond. I am here for those things, as are you," she said.

"And Gem?"

"Gem came seeking warmth. You give her that, but Gem's true love is the sun. Remember that, Mr. Lawton."

"Please, call me Matthew."

"As you wish, Matthew." She stood, a framework of bone beneath the cloth animated by a bright soul. "We will not speak again," she said.

"Why not?"

"I've told you the secret. I had to live long enough to pass it on. Treasure it and live, Matthew. John Sangamon did not," said Rainbow.

"You told this to Jack?"

She walked away from the table. Matthew was tempted

to stop her, but he didn't know what to say. So much of her language was mystical and impossible to believe. Age and illness had undoubtedly affected her mind.

Nevertheless he was acutely saddened when news reached him four days later that Rainbow Harvester was dead. The chief medic listed her age at death as fifty-one, and her true name as Unknown.

The *Bedouin* coursed through the photosphere. This was a good dip. The collection cells filled and closed down, row after row, with no gaps or leaks to spoil Matthew's 100 percent vow.

The sensation was there. From the back of his calves to his solar plexus, Matthew felt the stirring, tingling force. It had always existed, he knew; this time it seemed stronger, clearer. The power of suggestion? Matthew did not believe in mysticism. Rainbow was old and ill. The sun was a nuclear furnace, working on a vast but simple scale. It was not a god.

His hand strayed to the com-band selector. It was set on band five, the home frequency of Icecube. He touched the selector panel and the numbers began to climb. Seven, eight, nine.

Why do this? Do you expect to hear the sun groan?

Ten, eleven, twelve—Matthew stopped. The selector only moved from one full band to the next. A small wheel beside the panel allowed the pilot to fine-tune each band, eliminating interference. Matthew thumbed the little serrated wheel forward. Decimals appeared on the readout.

Twelve point two. Twelve point four. At twelve point five the selector locked on a signal.

The sun *does* moan.

Matthew's hair would have bristled, had it not been closely flattened by the tight heatsuit. The sound coming over the half band was not a voice. It resembled an old-style carrier wave in the bass register. A note would sound, descend the scale, stop, then start with the dying note of the last scale and repeat the process. Matthew imagined a man humming while descending a staircase.

"Spontaneous radio emissions," he said aloud. "Overlapping the com-band wave." He uttered this theory like a prayer, for he didn't want to believe what Rainbow said was true. He needed to hate the sun. It made him sharp and watchful. It kept him alive. What pleasure would there be in stealing the sun's power if it turned out to be a benevolent deity after all?

CHAPTER 11

"Are you ready?" called Sian from the bathroom.

"Yes," said Matthew impatiently. "What's the big surprise?"

"Wait, here I come!"

She emerged from the hall, planted her feet in the carpet, and threw her arms apart. "Ta-da!" she crowed.

Matthew had acquired a twin sister. Sian's hair was as white as Matthew's, and somewhere she'd managed to find skin dye dark enough to imitate his own russet coloring. The effect was startling.

Sian said, "What do you think?" She dropped her hands to her hips and turned around so Matthew could admire the evenness of the dye job.

"Is it permanent?" he said.

Her face fell. "You don't like it!"

"No, it's wild. I was just wondering if you're going to look like this the rest of your life."

"Don't be silly. A few pills and a Hydrop rinse, and I'll be bland old Sian Donnelly once more," she said.

Matthew smiled and put his arms around her. Her buttocks were still damp. "You are many things, Miss Donnelly, but you are not bland," he said.

"Sometimes you know exactly what to say," said Sian.

The guests began dropping from the sky an hour after sunset. Big, bulky skimmers rumbled over Matthew's roof and disgorged a gang of loud, boisterous people: Sian's co-workers from Triangle Photech.

Sian greeted them on the roof, which she had carefully lit so each new arrival would notice her hair and skin. Matthew stayed below in the living room, smiling and mumbling banalities at the strangers who came down the stairs.

The skimmers were sent down the valley to a parking pad. By the time the last vehicle was dispatched, Matthew was host to more than sixty people. Sian stood by his arm and introduced them as they made the obligatory orbit around their host. Matthew quickly lost track of them and remembered only a blur of first names and limp handshakes.

Charlie. Alicia. Graham. Faye. Pablo. Mikko. On and on, until Matthew met one who commanded more attention.

"Darling, I want you to meet Cassini Brooks," said Sian. He knew the name. Brooks was a particle engineer. He had designed the excellent dissipator units in Matthew's ship, *Aztec*.

"Call me Cass," he said, clasping Matthew's hand firmly.

"Pleased to meet you, Cass. I've wanted to tell you how well your units have performed in my ship," said Matthew.

"That's good to hear. It's rare I get feedback from an actual user," he said. "Have you experienced any static discharges during the fold-down phase?"

"None at all. The ion shedders compensate beautifully for any build-up."

Sian yawned ostentatiously. "No more shop talk!" she said. "Cass, go seduce one of the involved women." She pushed the handsome engineer away, and the crowd swallowed him.

"Hell, Shy. I finally meet someone I can talk to, and you send him away," Matthew complained.

"You don't want to be friends with him," said Sian. "Cass Brooks has the worst reputation in the Triangle as a ladykiller." She lowered her voice and put her lips close to his ear. "He's been after me for months."

"Has he ever caught you?"

"I won't say. Think about it awhile," she whispered. Sian touched the tip of her tongue to Matthew's ear and slipped away, laughing.

The music volume went up and the sociables went down. Food and fun drugs vanished into mouths, washed down by various mixtures of alcohol. Matthew circled the room twice, garnering three propositions en route—two from women. He heard all the usual questions about sundipping, and all the usual innuendos about the Gift. Men were as curious about it as women.

Mixing rapidly grew tiresome, and Matthew retreated to the kitchen. He kept watching for Sasha. Would she come?

The party spilled out onto the deck. Matthew hit the Teblights, and the blitzed celebrants ooh-aahed at the magnificent view down the mountain. The extra railing showed its worth when Richard Somebody-or-other fell from a chair while declaiming Admiral Torgov's Address in Solarian. The drunken orator bounced off the rail into the laps of an intimate threesome seeking privacy in a darker corner of the porch.

Matthew nursed a deep glass of rum and bay leaf at the

kitchen table. He was picking a bit of leaf from his teeth when he heard a voice say: "I am here, Matthew."

Sasha stood in the doorway, hands clasped in front of her. She wore a simple ankle-length gown, tied at the waist and devoid of holoid designs. Her long, straight hair was neatly combed. It fell across her neck and shoulders in a soft curve, the dark brown standing out against the light gray fabric of her dress.

"I'm glad," said Matthew.

She sat down at the table. "It was difficult getting here," she said. "A man had to help me up the ladder. He was very pleasant to me. Everyone present has been very kind to me."

"Everyone's blasted," said Matthew. Sasha looked puzzled. "Everyone's intoxicated," he said.

"You are not."

"I don't want to be. I wanted to be able to talk to you."

Sasha looked past him into space. "Matthew, there are many things you do not understand. I sense you feel strongly toward me. You must not. I cannot be intimate with you. It is not possible."

"How do you know till you try?" he said, not realizing the implicit admission he was making. "For some reason I feel drawn to you. I can't explain it, but I feel it all the same."

"It is because—" Sasha began. Sian tripped in the door.

"Ah-ha!" she said. Her face was glowing under the dye. "This must be the mysterious neighbor."

Matthew said, "Sian, meet Sasha."

Sian looped a wild strand of white hair behind her ear as she looked Sasha up and down.

"What a totally primitive presentation," she said. "Is this what arouses you these days, Matt? hildlike simpliss-simplicity?"

Matthew gripped his glass tightly. "You're being offensive, Shy. Take some Sting and sober up."

"The hell I will. I'm having a *good* time," she said. She grabbed Sasha by the arm and dragged her to the door.

"Come along, Sasha dear. I have someone you gotta meet. Someone interesting. Talking to Matt will bore you senseless. It's not what he does best!" she said. Sasha allowed herself to be hauled away without a word. Matthew cut the top off another liter of rum and mixed himself another large drink.

He drank it fast, his irritation increasing with each swallow. When the sodden leaves sank to the bottom of the empty glass, he marched out of the kitchen to find Sasha.

The party had dissolved into a dozen or so small groups, each centered around some particular activity. There was a political group, a music group, a damn-the-aliens group, etc. Snacks and pills were scattered over the carpet, and someone had taken Gem's holoid off the wall. Matthew replaced it and scanned the living room for Sasha. She was not there.

He tried the revival room. The light was off, but the hall globe cast a beam inside. Matthew heard breathing and got a glimpse of four feet. He shut the door and moved on. Another man lay face down in the shower stall, unconscious but breathing.

From his bedroom window Matthew saw her. Sasha was on the east end of the deck. Her back was to the rail, and a man had her penned there. A flush of jealous anger pushed Matthew to the one-way plexi. The man turned his head. Blue eyes and black hair: Cassini Brooks.

Cass was making time-honored entreaties in Sasha's ear, and she was listening earnestly. He stroked her bare arm, and she didn't object. Brooks touched his Ad-ban-wrapped knee against Sasha's thigh. She didn't avoid the contact. Matthew stood there, watching every step in a classic seduction, excited and angry and hurt at the same time. This was Sian's doing. She had aimed Sasha at Brooks, or Brooks at Sasha; it didn't matter. Damn her! And damn goddamn brilliant Cassini Brooks!

"Enjoying the show?" said Sian. She was there, slumped between the bed and the wall, watching him.

"Sometimes I hate you," she went on, "because you don't love me anymore. Did you ever, Matt? Even a little bit?"

"No," he said, for cruelty's sake.

"Bastard. You want her so bad I can see it from here." Sian rose unsteadily and came to him. "You won't get her, mister, not tonight. Cass will. He's already got her. Look!"

Matthew turned back to the window. Brooks had one arm around Sasha's waist and the other hand on her breast; he was kissing her. He was doing his best, eyes closed and lips moving, but Sasha was merely passive. Her eyes were wide and alert.

"Don't think about her, Matt. Think about me," said Sian. She laid her head on his back and circled his chest with her arms. "Right now. Right here."

He was smoldering. "What about the guests?"

"Let 'em get their own lay," she said.

He held her face roughly and kissed her hard. Sian tugged at the zipseams of his jersey until she felt skin. Over his shoulder Sian saw Brooks and Sasha climbing down the ladder to the ground. Matthew's house was too crowded for them. They were going to her place.

Matthew drew back long enough to rasp, "Lock the door."

Sian thrust her hands under the waist of his trousers. "No," she said.

"At least close it!"

She said, "I don't care if it's open or shut." In the end, neither did he.

Sian's breath brushed across his eyelids. Matthew opened his eyes and sought the wall chronograph. 03:18.

He slipped Sian off carelessly. She was blitzed beyond sensibility and slept on. Matthew pulled on his clothes, wincing now and then from the long scratches Sian had given him.

Three quarters of the guests were gone. The remainder were passed out all over the house. The audion had shut off the music and most of the lights. As Matthew picked his way through the living room, the audion detected him and spoke.

"Sir, I don't wish to be critical, but your guests have been most untidy," it said.

"Bunch of damned animals," said Matthew.

"Exactly so, sir. For example—"

"Save it. Is there anyone in the revival room?"

"Checking . . . infrared scan reveals it clear. Do you need medical attention, sir?"

"No, I want to use the telaudion," he replied.

Matthew's purpose was less than noble. He was burning to know if Brooks was still at Sasha's and if he had gained what Matthew desired most.

He opened the link and began scanning her house. Immediately he heard Sasha's strange music:

> Kissing in the dark—
> Not like dancing or walks in the park,
> It's something that all lovers do,
> Except for me and you.

He searched every room that had a terminal. Unfortunately, this did not include the pantry, upstairs bathroom, or the second-floor walk-in closet. Matthew asked for a directional grid from the three downstairs terminals and located the source of the music. The pantry.

A weird place to listen to archaic analog recordings, but then Sasha was a weird woman.

The night was cold. Matthew padded across the sharply sloping ground to Sasha's house. Luna was full, and he could see every feature of Sasha's tall, cylindrical dwelling looming above him with perfect clarity. The air was so still that the faint music reached him before he climbed onto her porch.

In the barren living room, Matthew found disturbing things. A man's shoes. A man's set of Ad-bans. Very expensive keff-cloth underwear.

Nat King Cole—or was it Perry Como?—crooned one song after another. It took Matthew an eternity to creep to the kitchen. The pantry door was ajar.

A feeble grayish light shone from a portabeam on a pantry shelf. Cass Brooks lay supine on the pantry floor, naked. His arms were flung wide and his knees were bent. It was his eyes that arrested Matthew; Cass's were rolled back in his head. Only white showed between his half-closed lids.

Sasha, her clothing undone and half gone, crouched on top of him, straddling his waist. One hand was planted, stiff fingered, over the man's heart. The other was reversed between Sasha's legs and dug deeply in the soft flesh over Cass's solar plexus. As Matthew stared in wonder, Brooks twitched feebly. Sasha threw her head back and shuddered. Cass spasmed harder, and Sasha shivered in unison.

This is not sex, Matthew realized. This is something else.

He let go the breath he'd been holding so long. Sasha heard his gasp and looked up. Their eyes met, and Matthew cried out in astonishment. Her eyes, her human eyes, dangled by tendons from the corners of their sockets. In their place were stark octagonal organs of sight, streaked with deep black lines.

Matthew fled. He ran through the unlit living room and tripped twice on Brooks's clothing. He blundered to the porch and nearly fell over the rail. As he stumbled back to his own house, one thought hammered in his mind.

It might have been me. It might have been me!

CHAPTER 12

The thirty-fourth day of the fourth quarter, Concordat Year 133, was Matthew's twenty-seventh birthday. Gem discovered this by consulting the records audion, and when the *Bedouin* docked at the conclusion of Matthew's nineteenth dip, she and all the nonworking dippers greeted him in the lounge with singing.

He was already the "old man" of Icecube. He had four years on the next-oldest male dipper, and of the women only Gem was his age.

The dippers gave him a couple of foolish gifts. Vine and the men presented him with an elaborate seat cushion (which would never fit in the *Bedouin*). Laura Shapiro and the women of Icecube gave Matthew a ridiculously large vial of Ubartay oil, a Freyan unguent reputed to be an infallible aphrodisiac.

Matthew hefted the vial and nodded. He handed the oil to Vine. "Here, Mitch. You need this more than I do," he said. Vine turned red amid much laughter.

Matthew was too tired to linger for the festivities, but

they continued in his honored absence. Gem accompanied him to their cabin. He sat listlessly on the bunk, peeling the sweat-soaked heatsuit from his feet and legs.

"Hard trip?" said Gem.

"Very. The damn spicules were so thick you could walk on them."

"But you got one hundred percent."

"I did," he said. "I have to go out again in thirty-six hours, if I'm going to meet the contract with Island Omicron."

"How much did you sign on for?" asked Gem quietly. When she was annoyed, she always grew very quiet.

"One-hundred-fifty billion megawatts."

"Due when?"

"Three-hundred-seventy-five days," he said. His upper tunic slapped the floor wetly.

"That's too short a time," said Gem. "Why do you accept such contracts? It can't be for the money."

Matthew fell back heavily on the bunk. "I'll take a longer vacation when I've filled this order," he said.

Gem sat on the edge of the bunk. She rubbed a finger across Matthew's chest. His skin was coated with a fine layer of ash, the remnant of his own epidermis.

"How deep did you go this time?" she said.

There was no reason to lie. "Within twenty-thousand km of the convection zone," he said.

"Why have you been going so deep? Does it fill the cells faster? Is it less turbulent?"

He held her hand and closed his eyes. "I'm looking for a clue," he said.

"To what?"

"Something Rainbow told me before she died. A lot of it was crazy stuff, about God, the sun, and how the sun is a living thing. But there was more. Rainbow explained to me about the Gift. How all sundippers have it."

"Some more than others," said Gem.

"Yes. You and I, we're more than gifted. I have it because I dip deeply and linger for a full load. You have it for a less obvious reason. Maybe women absorb it more fully. Maybe you have a natural affinity for the power."

Gem squeezed his hand. "It's no mystery. I'm rich in the Gift because you regularly give yours to me. When we love, the power passes from you into me," she said.

Matthew sat up suddenly. "Of course! That's it!"

"Do you really want to find out where the Gift comes from, and what it's made of?" said Gem.

"Certainly. Don't you?"

"It doesn't matter to me. I've always known about the Gift. It's nothing new. Humankind has sensed its presence all through history. Men in ages past formed vague theories about it. They gave it different names: 'pneuma,' 'od,' 'vril,' 'orgone.' It's all the same power, Matt. The sun creates it deep in its core. The energy permeates the solar system, and the closer one gets to the source, the more densely it flows."

"But what is it? Radiation? Particles? Plasma? What's its wavelength? Speed? Penetrative characteristics—"

"Why concern yourself? You can't control it. It can't be isolated or refined. Life-energy cannot be bottled! Why try? To sell, as we sell the crude power of the photosphere?" said Gem.

"Yes! If this life-energy could be captured, it'd be the greatest therapeutic substance in medical history," said Matthew.

"You think impossible things, my love. We're further from the ability to harness the Gift than cavemen were from sundipping."

Matthew reclined again. "I have to know, Gem. No matter how subtle the source is, I'll find it," he said.

"Jack found it. Rainbow found it. It's called death," she said. "Don't scoff! All life is merely borrowed. In the end, it always returns to its origins. But I'm not ready to part with you, Matthew Lawton. Hold on with me." Gem pressed her warm cheek to his cold one.

"I will, Gem," he said.

He slept. Gem disturbed him before she left. He sat up on one elbow and saw her swathed in her heatsuit, ready to go.

"What number is this?" asked Matthew.

"This'll be my fourteenth dip," said Gem.

"Ah, you'll never catch up with me."

"I have compensations," she said. "I'm better looking."

"Get out," he snorted, throwing a pillow at her. Gem dodged and came to the bunk. She knelt and kissed Matthew on the forehead.

"Remember," she said at the cabin door.

"Remember what?"

"Just remember."

He never saw her again.

Gem's ship, *Topaz,* was an elegant but elderly craft. When she was long overdue, the story spread quickly that the old ship had broken up trying to climb yet again out of the sun's ferocious grip.

Matthew didn't believe it. He flew the *Bedouin* in close solar orbit, searching for a crippled but intact *Topaz.* After sixty orbits, he switched to sweeping the surface of Mercury for wreckage. He found nothing.

The official period passed, and Gem Goldshield was declared dead. The dispersal of her station privileges began. Matthew refused to accept any of her shop time, fuel credits, or docking schedules. He made it difficult for anyone else to get Gem's privileges either.

Mitchell Vine claimed her fuel allowance. Matthew barred his way to the dispensing area.

"Move, Lawton. You've no right to interfere," said Vine.

"The hell I don't. You're not having her fuel. Gem's rights are forfeit. Nobody gets them," said Matthew.

"Don't be crazy. It's the way things are. If I got fried, you'd take some of my perks, wouldn't you?"

"Yeah, and you'd get part of mine. But not Gem's! Gem wasn't like you or me. I won't have her possessions picked over!"

Vine was young, impatient, and strong. He shook his head sadly and turned as if to go. With one lightning motion, he aimed a rolling punch at Matthew's face with every intention of apologizing once he had the fuel transferred to his account.

Matthew was distraught, but he wasn't comatose. He slipped under the fist and lowered his shoulder. Catching Vine under his raised arm, he carried the younger man bodily through the open doorway into the lounge. Vine hit the floor with Matthew on top of him.

"Get off!" Vine yelled. Matthew backhanded him across the face once, twice, and had drawn back for a third when someone stayed his hand. In a fury, Matthew turned to see who had stopped him.

"Let him up," said Arne Dawlish. Matthew saw Vine's blood on his knuckles and his rage turned to shame. He stood up and walked away, leaving Arne to tend the unconscious man.

Vine wasn't seriously hurt, but nary a word ever passed between him and Matthew again. The whole fight proved to be for nought, as the Icecube central audion broke up Gem's holdings and distributed them. Mitchell Vine got her fuel, and ever after nursed a hatred for Matthew.

The camaraderie of the sundippers was soured. Ironically, the man who had first fostered it was now the one who ruined it.

CHAPTER 13

It took an entire day for Matthew's house to recover from the party. The audion's manipulators picked and cleaned, straightened and wiped. Matthew lolled on the deck, keeping out of the machine's way.

Sian's friends revived one by one and crept away with mumbled words: thanks or apologies according to their fogged perceptions of the time they had. They were so slow in going Matthew made each sober person take at least one drunk with them. In this way he gradually put his house in order.

Sian remained. It was late afternoon when she crawled from Matthew's bed to the bathroom. He heard the jet running as she filled the tub. Sian stayed in the bath for an hour.

Matthew mixed a raw egg with orange juice and took it to her. Sian was submerged in steaming water up to her chin. A wet cloth covered her eyes. She didn't stir when he entered and sat down on the rim of the tub.

"Here," he said, holding out the juice. Sian groped blindly for the glass. Half the contents were gone before she paused for air.

"God," she croaked. "I feel awful."

"It shows," he said kindly. He noticed a string of dark bruises along her upper arms. They had been very rough on each other.

Matthew traced the bruises carefully. Sian said, "If there's any justice in the universe, you feel as bad or worse than I do."

"About what?"

"Last night. Everything."

"It'd be hard to say who behaved the worse," said Matthew.

"Call it a draw," she said. Sian gulped the rest of the cold juice. Matthew plucked the empty glass from her nerveless fingers.

"Where'd you go early this morning?" asked Sian. "I felt you leave while it was still dark."

"Out. I went—out. For fresh air."

"A short walk 'round the mountain at three A.M.?" She sighed. "Jesus, Matt; I'm not stupid. Did you find Sasha?"

"I saw her, yes."

"With Cass?"

"Yes."

"I told you he was a ladykiller," said Sian.

Yes, thought Matthew, *and he got more than he bargained for.* "I don't want to talk about Sasha," he said. "I want to talk about us. I'm sorry about last night, Shy."

She lifted the damp rag from her face. A feverishly bloodshot eye peeked out at him. "Things must be bad," she said. "You've never apologized to me for anything. This woman seems to've really shaken you."

"It's not her. It's a lot of things."

"Like screaming nightmares and Crux ampules and

someone called Gem?" said Sian. Matthew's face contorted for a second. Sian lifted a hand from the soapy
water and laid it on his knee.

"Who is Gem?" she asked gently.

"Was. She's dead. Lost in the sun two years ago," he
said.

"She must be the one," said Sian. Matthew asked what
she meant. "The one whose picture is on the living room
wall. The one who's still with you, even when we make
love. Was she so special?"

"Unique is the word I'd use," he said. "A rare person,
Gem; her only vice was a blind belief in fate."

He went on to describe in short, careful sentences his
early days with Gem Goldshield and Jack Sangamon.
When he was done, Sian was crying. Matthew was dry
eyed and detached.

"I wish I'd never met you," Sian said. "I'll never be
able to share your past, or be part of your life in space."
She sniffed loudly and rubbed her glistening nose. "Worst
of all, I'll never be the one you call to in your dreams."

"I tried," said Matthew. He stood. "I wanted you to be
special, too. It just didn't happen."

He closed the bathroom door quietly. He crossed the
hall to his bedroom, lay down, and listened to Sian weep.

Sasha's house was deadly still. No music. No sounds of
breathing. Cass Brooks's clothing no longer littered the
floor. No evidence.

Matthew mounted the spiral stairs. His hard-sole shoes
clacked on the uncarpeted treads. He followed the cold
concrete path to Sasha's room. The door was slightly
ajar.

Sasha lay curled up on a rough rectangle of concrete.
She was asleep, and did not waken when Matthew entered. He walked around her, studying her. She was clad
in a loose, coverall-type garment of yellow cotton. Sasha's

sides moved in easy rhythm, and her lips were moist with saliva.

You're crazy, Lawton. Sasha Mackensen is human. Look at her—eyelashes, fine downy hair on her neck, calluses on her toes. What you saw last night was the result of too much rum and mental tension. It's called paranoia.

He leaned against the wall to think. There were cases of aliens who tried to pass themselves off as humans. Most often these were Freyans looking for jobs on Earth. Could Sasha be Freyan? It seemed unlikely. Disguised aliens always wore heavy makeup and silicone prostheses. Sasha wore neither. Aliens usually exaggerated what they perceived as normal human characteristics. Sasha behaved too strangely to avoid attention.

He couldn't resolve the data. Matthew slowly slid down the wall to wait for Sasha to awaken. He waited a long time. The sun set and the room went gray before she moved.

She saw him. "Hello," she said.

"You don't seem surprised to see me," he said.

"I expected you. Why did you let me sleep?"

"It was easier to observe you that way."

"And what have you learned?"

"You're perfect. You're the most perfect human imitation I've ever seen," he said.

"Thank you. I have had doubts from time to time."

"You admit it?"

"Yes. I am not a human."

Matthew put his hand in his jacket pocket. Out came a small (and strictly illegal) plasmer pistol.

"Do you intend to kill me?" asked Sasha.

"Only if you make it necessary. Mainly this is for my protection. If you killed David Mackensen and Cassini Brooks, I don't want to join them," said Matthew.

"Cass is not dead. He left for the Triangle this morning."

"But I saw—"

"You saw a very intimate, unrecognizable process and assumed the worst," she said. The shy, confused-girl pose was gone. Matthew saw he was dealing with an intelligent and resilient personality.

"Who are you?" said Matthew.

"A stranger."

"You're not one of the Concordat races," he said.

"I am from far, far outside the boundaries of the Concordat. Though I have studied star charts and navigational holoids, I cannot find my home star. I am truly lost."

Sasha stood. Matthew kept the tip of the plasmer on her as she went to the window.

"I came here nine years ago. I was rescued in deep space by an Earth vessel. Before I was found, I met another spacewreck victim, a human, and from him I fabricated the shell you see now," said Sasha. Matthew shook his head in confusion. She explained, "Using samples of human blood, skin, semen, and nerve tissue, I altered the genetic structure of my outer body to resemble *homo sapiens*. As I knew I had no chance to return to my own world, I was forced into disguise in order to live in yours."

Sasha touched a fingertip to the plexi pane. "A strange world, this Earth. Everything is divided. Air and land; land and water. Plants and animals. Male and female," she said.

"Aren't you female?" said Matthew.

"No. I took this form because it afforded me better opportunities to satisfy my hunger."

A distant glimmer of recognition entered Matthew's mind. "When I saw you with Cass, it wasn't sexual. You were feeding. Is that it?"

"Exactly, Matthew. My kind subsists on energy, preferably biological," she said. "This division of humans into male and female sexes allows me to approach men for my own purposes."

"Dinner comes to you, like Cass last night."

"It is not an easy thing to do," she said. "Feeding has a draining effect on the subject, but it is not lethal if done in moderation. The difficulty arises in the emotional response of the human male. The act of feeding provokes an intense neurological reaction."

"You mean it feels good?" said Matthew.

"Yes. Though no actual sexual contact is made, the subject experiences a powerful reaction in the brain similar to a prolonged orgasm," said Sasha. She cast her eyes to the floor. "There is also a feedback effect. The more intensely a subject responds, the greater the drain of life from him to me. Until I learned to control myself, I harmed several humans seriously."

"Is that what happened to Mackensen?"

"Yes."

"You called him your husband. Was he?"

"In the legal sense. He wanted to marry me. I acquiesced to his wishes."

"Surely he knew what you were!"

"He knew. David and I met at Canaveral spaceport three years ago. I was in a desperate situation, trying to leave the planet. A man I'd fed from had tracked me down with the intention of exposing me. The memory of the experience stayed with him, and I was able to trick him into feeding me again. I deliberately went too far and drained all life from him.

"The constabulary called it murder and began to hunt me. I was preparing to flee when David Mackensen found me. Like you, he was attracted to me, and offered to help. I knew this response well; males can seldom resist a female in distress.

"He took me to his home in Baltimore. After a short period of verbal persuasion, David attempted to force a sexual act on me."

"The truth must've been quite a shock," said Matthew.

"Do you know what his reaction was? Delight. His first thought upon finding I was not human was to have me taken to a laboratory and vivisected for scientific purposes. Then I demonstrated my feeding technique to him and he changed his mind," said Sasha.

"I'll bet."

"David was advanced in age and seldom capable of normal sexual relations. As my effects are strictly neurological, he was able to derive strong pleasure from them without physical exertion. A symbiotic relationship formed. As a high official in the Beneficial Party, he was able to give me shelter and protection. I, in turn, fed on his biological energy and gave him pleasure he could not derive any other way."

"Sounds very cozy," said Matthew. "So how did Mackensen die?"

"His position in the Party was a strain for him. He was constantly battling ambitious subordinates who sought to partition his authority among themselves. Our marriage came about because other Party officials claimed it was improper for a man of David's status and age to live with a young mistress.

"The stress drove David to seek my attentions with increasing frequency. I warned him I was draining his life away. He did not care. He said I was the only source of pleasure in his life, and he was not going to curtail it. I had no option. I was slowly killing him, and he demanded more and more.

"Soon he was bedridden. Party members gathered around and boasted to his face how they were planning to replace him. Their cruelty amazed me. Is it a function of politics, Matthew, or are all humans innately cruel?"

He shrugged. "It's in all of us, I guess. Comes from being weak and fearful."

Sasha said, "I kept away from David for several days, but he worsened regardless. I knew he was going to die. I formed a plan to escape. Using David's audion, I found this house. It was remote and expensive, so I believed no one would look for me here. I intended to take a large sum of currency with me to use to persuade local authorities to ignore me.

"Everything would have gone well had David lived two days longer. He died too soon. The Party confiscated his house and property for beneficiation. My fate was in the hands of his political successor, a woman named Erica Taylor. Pro Taylor tried to force me to relinquish David's inherited property to her. I refused. She locked me in my room, but I escaped with David's chauffeur and came here. The Party is still looking for me, ostensibly in connection with David's death, but in fact because Pro Taylor needs me to legitimize her claims to David's wealth and power."

Matthew put the plasmer back in his pocket. He got to his feet and went to the window.

"What about me? Was the coy act designed to lure me closer or keep me away?" he said.

Sasha turned and looked up at him. "I did not want you near. It was dangerous for me. You might have been a Party member. As time passed I grew hungry. You were an obvious source of sustenance. I decided not to encourage you, but to take advantage of any opportunities your interest presented."

"And the storm? The kiss?"

"Accidents. My world does not have natural discharges of energy like your lightning. Storms are excruciating for me. Electricity is much like the biological energy in humans, and massive aerial discharges can seriously disable me," she said.

Sasha raised her left hand and rested her fingers on Matthew's chest. "When you kissed me, I thought: my hunger is ended. But as I made initial contact, I found a source of great energy within you. I have not encountered such energy before. Contact with it was very painful."

"We call it the Gift," said Matthew. "Sundippers get it working inside the sun's photosphere. Some claim it's pure life-energy."

"Perhaps so. All I know is, I cannot feed from you, Matthew. To do so would hurt me."

Matthew put a hand to Sasha's cheek. No one would suspect, looking at that simple, appealing face, that it wasn't human.

"You have no sex at all?" he said in a very low voice.

"I have no reproductive functions," said Sasha.

"Pity."

"I agree," she said, for entirely different reasons. They remained there, millimeters apart, each wanting from the other something they could not get.

CHAPTER 14

"What's that thingum for?" asked Chief Mechanic Arne Dawlish. He was about to secure Matthew in the *Bedouin* for his twenty-first dip when he noticed a bulky techno-tronic package mounted on the floor between the pilot's feet.

"A special detector," said Matthew.

"For what? Sunspots?"

"No, hot spots. I've been going deep lately, and I want to locate convection columns rising before I fly right through them."

A plausible lie. All Icecube knew Matthew was dipping deeper and deeper into the photosphere. No one was sure why, because Matthew wasn't talking. Since Gem's loss he'd withdrawn from his colleagues, mixing with them very little.

Some believed Matthew was looking for Gem. There was a persistent myth that far down in the photosphere there existed cool zones, places where the temp was no higher than the brightside of Mercury. Dippers who vanished were often said (facetiously) to be vacationing in the Cool Zone. Many of the greats were there: Momar, Gerri Hill, Daze Chromo—and Gem Goldshield.

In an oddly etiological way, Matthew *was* searching for Gem. The lash-up device in the *Bedouin* was a selective emanation detector. He had made it himself. Its purpose was to find the source of the Gift.

Dawlish dogged down the cupola. Matthew switched to internal power and boosted *Bedouin* away from the space station. The voice of Ahmad, his audion, warned him he had only three point five minutes to rendezvous with the Fire Truck.

"I'm not using the Truck," said Matthew.

"Is that advisable, sir? The temperature of the corona is very high," said Ahmad.

"I have it on good authority that it's mostly harmless. Besides, I want to scan the corona as we pass through it."

Instead of a chasing orbit to the brightside of Mercury, Matthew swung the *Bedouin* out in retrograde solar orbit.

"Lay in a course A-forty-sixty-six, tangential," he instructed the audion. "We're giving him a close shave today."

"Who, sir?" said Ahmad. Anthropomorphism was not part of his program.

"I'm putting it over," said Matthew. Keeping the stubby joystick in a wide starboard turn, Matthew reached between his knees and activated the detector. The hemispherical display glowed, and numbers tracked across the bottom of the screen. If any energy sources within the suspected band (above cosmic rays) were discovered, concentric rings would appear on the display, focusing on the origin of the emanation.

"Contact with the corona in eight seconds," said Ahmad.

Despite the instrument buffers, *Bedouin*'s gauges leaped off their scales as Matthew plunged into the corona. The spectroscope showed the temp of the gas outside climbing past one million degrees Kelvin. Yet the ship's skin remained a tolerable 4,285 K. Rainbow was right. The corona was too tenuous to be thermally harmful.

On the other hand, the radiation levels were definitely unhealthy. Matthew shifted uneasily in his seat, as if feeling every particle passing through his ship and his body, setting the stage for all kinds of future cellular mischief.

The *Bedouin* flew well. Shielding, coolant, and dissipators performed efficiently. As the denser chromosphere approached, Matthew felt confident enough to put on some music. To match his mood, he chose something dark and menacing: Mahler's First Symphony, the *Titan*.

The only indication Matthew observed upon entering the chromosphere was a steady decrease in the ambient temp. This went down to only ten thousand K, but the ship's skin temp shot up to meet this figure. The cooling systems labored to defend the human pilot from the thermal onslaught. The maximum temp the *Bedouin* was claimed able to withstand was twelve thousand K. Not much of a margin.

The special detector remained passive. Matthew swept the surface of the sun to the greatest radius of the device and found nothing. The disturbance caused by ionizing hydrogen in the chromosphere overloaded the other instruments. In the last few thousand kilometers, cosmic ray and gamma counters failed.

The dipper ship sliced into the heavier layers of the photosphere at high speed. Matthew was immediately caught in a surge of tidal force. He rotated the stick in the direction of the flow and let the whirlpool fling him out to calmer regions.

"Open collection cells," he said. The array panel blinked with activity as Ahmad supervised the filling of the power packs. The cells were forty-eight percent full when a dark ring appeared on the detector display. The machine emitted a deep bass hum. Matthew leaned forward so fast he tore the musicon lead from his ears.

"Ahmad, coordinate this pattern," he said.

"Sir, the cells are not yet full. Shouldn't I—"

"Do what I say! Find the pattern!"

A grid was superimposed on the display. Ahmad said, "The heliocenter of the phenomenon lies on bearing two-five-two by oh-six-one. The source is receding at eight hundred twenty-two kph."

"Receding? How?"

"As we traverse the photosphere at one hundred eight thousand nine hundred forty-five kph, the source of these emanations is receding deeper into the sun some eight hundred twenty-two kph in excess of our speed," said Ahmad.

"Go after it. Dive!"

The *Bedouin* slanted down and gained velocity. A bead of sweat trickled over Matthew's eyebrow and stung his left eye. The heat, pressure, and gravity outside were enough to reduce him to a wisp of vapor. The ship's systems struggled to keep their master alive as he pursued the fading clue deeper into the sun.

"Target receding at one thousand one hundred fifty-six kph. Shall I increase our rate of descent?" said Ahmad.

"How far are we from the convection layer?"

"Subsounding indicates twelve thousand two hundred km."

The ring on the display shifted. With astonishing speed, the source of the emanation passed under the *Bedouin* and raced away.

Matthew screwed the ship in a murderous turn. Ahmad reported general failures of a dozen functions.

"Never mind," said Matthew. "Let everything go but engine and life support systems. Understand?"

"Yes, sir. What about the energy already collected?" said the audion.

"Dump it. Tap it out."

Ping, ping, went the detector. The source was rising toward them. Matthew had no visual display, of course, so he could only follow the target on instruments. The source was hundreds of kilometers wide and shapeless. Most likely it was a self-contained field of energy, analogous to ball lightning. If Matthew could get close enough, he intended to fly into it and trap what portion he could in his collector cells.

He lost com-band communications to a transfer overload. The inboard repulsors flared and were gone. Bits of the *Bedouin* burned away as the target rose within seven hundred km of the ship.

"Ahmad, listen closely. When I call for it, I want you to give me a two second burst of full engine thrust. Got that?"

"On what heading, sir?"

"Any heading out of the sun."

"You wish to flake, sir?"

"If the worst happens, yes," said Matthew. "Flake and take the ship home."

"Yes, sir," said Ahmad.

The target was ahead and slightly below, traveling at 114,072 kph. Matthew's finger strayed over the manual switch for opening the cell array. Time seemed to stretch out to infinity as the evasive target rose centimeter by centimeter to Matthew's level. He was afraid to dive at it, afraid the ship's impetus would alert it and send it scurrying away.

Wait, wait. Let it come to you.

The detector locked, and the target ring expanded to fill the display. Matthew nudged the *Bedouin* forward and opened the cells.

A strange, cooling sensation ran over his skin. Gradually he noticed the normally dark control module was suffused with a clear blue light. Matthew held out his hand and saw it was sheathed in the same azure glow. He looked down and realized his fluorescing body was illuminating the module.

His extremities were ice cold, and his limbs trembled with increasing violence. He tried to speak, but the cold effluvium blocked his vocal cords.

Several different things began to happen at once. Matthew's voluntary body functions began to act on their own. Tears ran down his face. He rapidly filled his urine and waste bags. His vision blurred and sharpened, his nose ran, and his teeth chattered. A sharp pain over his stomach spread down his abdomen. It reached his testicles, and Matthew nearly passed out.

This is what it feels like. Gem and Rainbow were right. The source of life is also the source of death.

He tried to order Ahmad to flake, but no sound issued from his throat. There was one thing left to try. Hit the Crux ampule. Doing so automatically alerted the audion that the pilot was incapable of further flying.

Matthew lifted his arm from the velpad. It wavered wildly as he tried to control it. The blue shimmer was blinding now, and fine strands of light curled back from his fingertips to his wrists. With tremendous effort of will, he brought the heel of his hand down hard on the hypnotic drug ampule.

There was no sensation of breaking glass, no prick of microbores into the flesh of his thigh. In a horrifying second of insight, Matthew wondered if the drug would work while his body was filled with the unknown energy.

The interior of the *Bedouin* faded from view. A series of images started flashing in Matthew's brain. Crux hallucinations? Or another effect of the concentrated Gift?

He saw people he knew, places he'd been. Though each picture lasted only as long as a synaptic discharge, it seemed to Matthew as if years were passing. Trouble was, the images were not in chronological order.

Jack Sangamon taking a high-low pot both ways. Tycho Basin, on Luna, where he grew up. Gem smiling in the rescue pogo. His mother and father, arguing. Gem reclining nude in their Icecube cabin. The house on Buncombe Horse Range Ridge. Wellington Yu, fat and legless. Gem kissing him. Jack in his heatsuit. Tranquility University. Rainbow Harvester as he never saw her, without her hood. Her face was a sea of tumors, black and hideous. Behind that awful mask was the most serene mind in the solar system.

Gem. Gem dancing with Jack. Gem at orgasm. Gem eating noodles. Gem.

The synaptic flashes lost coherence and became mere bursts of cerebral light. It was as if a strobe were fixed in Matthew's skull, firing in sequence with his brain waves. His conscious mind let go.

Faithful Ahmad flaked the *Bedouin* as he was programmed and carried his master to the safety of open space.

CHAPTER 15

"Tell me about your world," said Matthew.

"That is difficult," said Sasha. "So much of my native planet cannot be expressed vocally. We do not have oral communication, and I suspect the similes I might make would be grossly inadequate."

"If your kind don't talk, how do you communicate?" asked Matthew.

Sasha made vague gestures with her hands. "You might say 'empathy,' but this is imprecise. Our senses are not separated into distinct functions, such as humans' are. Our nervous systems detect the brain activity of others, and in this fashion we speak to one another."

"Hmm, telepathy. Can you read my mind that way?"

"It does not work with humans. Your nerve impulses are too weak to escape your body. Also, clothed as I am in human flesh, I am less sensitive than I used to be."

Matthew leaned against the wall. "There's so much I want to know. You're a new species, totally unlike the other races in the Concordat."

Sasha replied, "As I said, men are perpetually curious." She looked at the palm of her hand. "There is a way I can show you my world."

"Then do it."

"I warn you, Matthew. It will require an intimacy of contact you may find disturbing," she said.

"Will it hurt?"

"No, but it may be psychologically uncomfortable, and you may find the method itself physically repellent."

His interest was too great to back away now. Matthew still desired close contact with Sasha, even if it wasn't sexual.

He followed her down to the kitchen. The cabinets were full of cooking utensils, and Sasha rummaged around until she found a small, sharp paring knife. As Matthew looked on, she dug the tip of the blade into the palm of her left hand.

"What're you doing?" he said.

Sasha said nothing. She made an incision two and a half centimeters long in her palm. Then she crossed the cut with another of equal length. Matthew noticed a few drops of red blood seep from the wound. She wiped it clean, and it bled no more.

Sasha flexed her fingers back and bent her wrist to tighten the skin on her hand. A small, cone-shaped piece of flesh protruded through the cut. She stared at the bright yellow bud intently. It lengthened as she concentrated, growing out of her palm with gentle circular undulations.

"What is that?" said Matthew in horrified fascination.

"A specialized extrusive nerve," said Sasha, "both inductive and conductive. We will communicate through it."

He couldn't avert his gaze from the waving tendril. "How is it done?" he said faintly.

"I must make contact with a major sensory nerve," she said. "Through the ear or behind the eye is best."

"And then I'll hear or see what your brain generates for me?"

"Yes. Which would you prefer?"

He thought a moment. Reaching his auditory nerve would require breaking his eardrum. He said, "Can you reach my optic nerve without damaging my sight?"

Sasha ran a forefinger around Matthew's eyes. "The sockets are large," she said. "I can slip under your lid readily enough, but I am not certain I can get between the muscles surrounding the eye. Are you willing for me to try?"

"Yes," he said.

The postures were difficult to arrange. Sasha had to be very close to Matthew's face. There were no chairs, so the arrangement had to be done on the floor. Matthew sat down with his back against the wall. Sasha knelt over his lap and braced her right arm over his shoulder. Matthew laughed nervously.

"Two days ago I'd have given anything to get you in this position," he said. "Now that I'm here, I feel nervous as a virgin."

"Are you afraid?"

"I don't want my vision damaged."

"Don't worry, Matthew. I will be gentle."

He closed his left eye. She slowly brought the weird tendril to the right one. His blink reflex was constant, and Sasha couldn't get her tendril in. Finally she held his lids apart with her fingers.

The alien nerve, warm and slick, flattened as it worked its way under his eyelid. Matthew tried to stay calm, but the sensation of invasion was too strong. The muscles in his cheek clenched. Sasha gave a gasp of pain. The tendril was extremely sensitive.

"Shall I stop?" said Sasha. She sounded very far away, though her lips were only centimeters from his ear.

"No, I can handle it," he said. His cheek slowly

relaxed, and Sasha insinuated further into Matthew's skull.

The creeping sensation was almost more than he could bear. Matthew found himself gripping Sasha tightly by the hips. Whether it was their proximity, simple pressure, or the weird eroticism of the situation, Matthew was becoming excited. He forced his mind into other channels, such as keeping his facial muscles relaxed.

Contact. Warmth rushed down the right side of his face. A splotch of colors was painted on his retina from within, and the discomfort faded as Sasha drew it into herself.

A dark line resolved itself into a horizon. Matthew found himself looking at a flat, waveless ocean under a clear blue-green sky. His perspective turned, and he saw a rocky shoreline devoid of trees or other megaflora.

"This is my world," said Sasha. "In our language, it is called Alive. My race are Those Who Think, and our lives begin in the liquid you see around you."

"You're amphibians?" said Matthew.

"No. The body of liquid you see is not water; it is a complex suspension of proteins, amino acids, and photosensitive chemicals."

"Sounds like a living organism."

"It is, Matthew. It is the womb of my kind. Come." He descended into the dark green fluid. It parted thickly, almost like gelatin. Matthew thought he wouldn't be able to see below its surface, but he could. Luminous forms moved in and out of the gloom. Some swam through the soup, others walked on the bottom.

"Our early lives are a deep mystery," said Sasha. "Our origins are kept from us by Those Who Create. What I imagine for you now is based on dim memories of my larval life."

A short figure, wreathed in yellow light, trudged through the darkness. Its head was huge in proportion to its body. The legs were squat and powerful, as legs in this soup had to be. The arms were tiny, almost rudimentary. They dangled uselessly on either side of the flat, feature-less chest of the yellow creature.

"This is me as a larva," said Sasha.

Matthew looked more closely. The head was feature-less save for two angular eyesockets and a simple, lipless mouth shaped like a short, stiff tube.

"What do you breathe down here?" he asked.

"We do not breathe. All our life functions are sup-ported by the albumen around us."

"How long is the larval stage?"

"No one knows. We measure time in sleeps, or periods of rest, once we emerge from the albumen. Thus we have no measurement for the larval time," she said.

Matthew saw no sign of tool use or technological development. He mentioned this, and Sasha explained that larvae have very limited mental abilities. Since they don't have to worry about food, clothing, shelter, or protection, they tend to spend their time walking in the murk, sharpening their senses on the other creatures around them.

Another yellow figure appeared, coming toward the immature Sasha. Matthew had a sensation of being touched, even though the stranger was some meters away. He heard—or rather, felt—this message:

I am for you, I am for we, I am for us, I am for me.

Sasha sent back this reply: *You are for me, you are for we, you are for us, you are for you.*

"What does it mean?" said Matthew.

"Wait," said Sasha.

The stranger came nearer. Its arms were well devel-oped, and its head bore two curving crests from the mouth back over the eyes to the rear of the skull.

"This is an Almost-Emergent," said Sasha.

The creature held out its three-fingered hands and gathered the smaller Sasha to it. Its mouth tube covered Sasha's. The Almost-Emergent injected a bitter-tasting substance into the smaller being's mouth.

Matthew gagged. "What the hell was that?"

"This one is about to emerge. It is giving me a bacteria culture that separates oxygen from the albumen. Soon it will breathe air, and it must clear its pneumosac for that moment," she said.

The creature let go. It strode up the sloping bottom of the living sea. Its head broke the surface, and it marched onto dry land.

"This happens to all of you?" said Matthew. In answer, Sasha shifted forward in time. Now she had arms. She embraced a younger larva and expelled the germ culture from her gut into the other creature.

"Larvae will not mature without the bacteria from an Almost-Emergent," she said, "and only a larva with well-developed sensory skills can hear the call of an adult."

Sasha walked out of the green albumen. A crowd of brilliant yellow adults stood by the shore to greet her. Matthew felt their empathic thoughts showering on Sasha. They were beautiful, friendly thoughts, designed to make the Emergent feel welcome.

As the adult Sasha stood by the edge of the albumen sea, she began to shake herself and stamp her peglike feet. This, she told Matthew, was the emerging dance. It was meant to dislodge all droplets of the albumen, so the womb of the race would not be diminished.

The assembled adults praised Sasha's performance. *See how well the new one does the dance*, they sent. Sasha stopped and responded, *I will be Dance. I am Dance.*

"Was that your original name?" said Matthew.

"Yes, my emerging name."

"I like it. It suits you. Dance."

The adults escorted Sasha/Dance inland. Matthew discovered where bare rock was not exposed, a thick mat of living fiber covered the entire planet. This was the dry counterpart of the albumen sea, and in some places it was hundreds of meters deep. Bubbles of gas, chiefly oxygen, issued from the mat in great flatulent eruptions. Dance's people built walking platforms over the mats, so as not to sink into the syrupy growth.

Those Who Think didn't wear clothing. They didn't need it; the climate was balmy, and their bodies were innocent of external organs or vulnerable openings. As Matthew observed, the adult beings were completely sexless. Their bright yellow skins were smooth from their necks to their narrow feet. Only in the cavity between the bony ridges of the skull did they have any sort of hair.

"Dance, how do your kind reproduce?" he said.

"It happens in the depths of the albumen," she said. "We do not remember the process once we emerge. All we know is, the sexual function is lost long before the end of the larval stage."

The procession reached a modest-size settlement built on pilings above the organic mat. The houses, platforms, and pilings were made of a ribbed, plasticlike material. Matthew saw no metal in domestic use.

"You have a question," said Dance.

"I'm wondering. Things are so primitive here. How did you manage to travel so far across space on this level of technology?"

"It was not our doing," said Dance. The scene dissolved. A far larger city spread out before his view. Everything was tinted green, but Matthew couldn't tell if this was an innate effect of Dance's vision, or if the planet's sun was a blue series star.

"This was my home before the Others came," she said.

"Our culture was high. We knew no want, for we lived on the energy of the living mat and required no other sustenance. We pursued our arts to the neglect of the sciences, as we derived pleasure from the creation of beauty and harmony. But this life made us ill prepared to meet the arrival of the hHoma." She pronounced this with a sharp exhalation before the first syllable: *huh*-HO-maa.

"Who're they?" asked Matthew.

"Like your people, a race of star travelers. Through telescopes, we saw the arrival of a vast number of hHoma spaceships around our planet. Their scouts landed, and we greeted them with curiosity."

Matthew received a picture of a hHoma ship. Its prismatic surface resembled a bee's eye. The waffled exterior surface of the football-shaped craft hardly seemed conducive to interstellar flight.

The hHoma exited their machine, and Matthew's intense interest sharpened the scene. The hHoma were enormous froglike creatures, two-and-a-half meters tall. Their legs were short and squat, while their arms (forelegs?) were long enough to rest on the ground. Add to this a flat, triangular head and gray-green skin, and the frog illusion became very strong.

Dance said, "The hHoma were on a migratory trek to new worlds. Alive was the first planet in many sleeps they had found with a breathable atmosphere. We did not care if they settled, for the numbers of Those Who Think were never very large. The hHoma realized this, and soon began landing their people all over the planet. They were agreeable beings, if arrogant, and they regarded us as docile savages."

Matthew saw an immense structure of metal rise out of the flat terrain. This megastructure was a hHoma colony, and he soon saw thousands of the bulky creatures stumping about. They flew and rode in machines not too different from Concordat skimmers. Dance's race remained in the background, quiet, unassuming, and peaceful.

Things changed. The dense crowds of hHoma thinned. Dance said, "In a few years, many hHoma began dying. Their medicians theorized that a bacterium native to Alive was the cause. They worked furiously to isolate the suspected source and find a cure. It eluded them. The more time went by, the weaker the alien colonists became. Five years after the hHoma convoy landed, few still lived."

The mighty metal ziggurat returned to his sight, empty and pitted with corrosion. The moldy bones of hHoma lay scattered about its base. There was no one to bury them.

"One of the last hHoma was a creature named Lowthroat. He (for the hHoma are sexed as humans are) was not a scientist or a medician. He was an engineer," she said. Lowthroat appeared. He was stooped and bloated, and patches of iridescent slime glistened on his skin. By his own standards, Lowthroat was a very sick being.

"It was Lowthroat who discovered the cause of the mass dying. He was recording the levels of energy emitted by the organic mat and the albumen sea. There were plans to power hHoma machinery with this energy, but it was too low in intensity. Lowthroat noticed his readings always declined when one of my kind passed his sensor. He made an experiment. He planted an energy sensor in a remote place. It sent out regular signals as the fibers beneath it lived, grew, and multiplied. Then Lowthroat sent two of us to the spot. The probe sent weaker and weaker signals, then ceased.

"There was the answer. Those Who Think live by absorbing energy from other living things. Before the hHoma, the planet supported as many of my kind as it could—perhaps two hundred thousand as you count. The onset of the alien colonists upset this balance. All at once, there was more 'food' than before. More of our kind emerged from the albumen, and we drained the life from the hHoma colonists. We did not know what we were doing, nor could we stop it.

"Lowthroat sent a message to the hHoma space fleet. 'The natives have killed us,' he reported. Warships came to Alive to punish us."

In a round black field, such as one sees through an optical telescope, Matthew saw a horde of large space-ships converging on Alive.

"Our political organizations were too small and ineffective to organize resistance or offer negotiation. Moreover, there were now one million of us, and the planet could not support this population. Large tracts of the organic mat began to die as all life was taken from it. Those Who Think despaired. With no action on our parts, two grave threats faced us: death by violence and death by starvation.

"The hHoma attacked and killed thousands. Their weapons were all the more effective because the massive discharges of energy by their coherent light and proton beam devices killed even when they did not hit us. You recall how I reacted to the thunderstorm? This was a million times worse."

It was worse. Powerful ships, glittering like faceted gems, swept Alive with deadly rays. Those Who Think collapsed in droves. They were defenseless, and Matthew was sickened by the sight of so many beings incinerated for a crime they couldn't avoid.

His breath came hard. Anger and sadness pushed adrenalin through his body. He was learning empathy by feeling what Dance had experienced.

"The hHoma fleet flew away. Only a few thousand of Those Who Think survived. Great swaths of the organic mat had been destroyed, too, and it seemed to us who survived that we were doomed to extinction," she said.

"One alternative presented itself. We had many examples of hHoma technology around. I and my friends worked on several ships, making them spaceworthy. When the repairs were complete, we departed from Alive, intending to find new worlds to inhabit.

"It was a bold and dangerous venture. We knew nothing about space navigation, and soon lost our way in the unbounded void. The weakest among us died as food for the stronger. Now we were feeding on each other. It was a terrible time. I felt such guilt, for I did not want to drain them. The voyage continued until only two of us were left."

A dimly lit spacecraft speeded aimlessly through space. Matthew saw Dance and her companion. (He decided he couldn't think of Dance as anything but female.)

"We decided to separate. I left in a scouting vessel. It flew automatically toward impulses it received that indicated sentient activity: radio signals, ion trails, and so forth. When my fuel was exhausted, I drifted into the area known as Abr Valley," she said.

"I know that region," said Matthew. "It's a frequently used stellar track between Shiva and Kaltha."

"The zone I drifted into was a place of many spacewrecks. I tried saving the alien creatures I found, but all died of their injuries. This was not altruism on my part. I needed a strong, living subject to draw energy from. I finally found one, a male human named Allen Gunther."

A man's face appeared to him. He was in his midtwenties, and Matthew could see where Dance acquired her features, if she had used genetic material from this man.

"Allen taught me what to expect should I live among humans. His life energies were potent and strange, but I found them palatable.

"The rest you know," said Dance. "My furtive life on

Earth, David Mackensen, and you. What do you think of
Sasha now?"

"Take the tendril out, will you?" he said. It slipped
free. Matthew worked his eyelid up and down. The used
orb was sore, and tears ran continuously down his cheek.

"Whew," he said. "What a jaunt!" Dance watched him
expectantly. He felt ridiculous, holding this not-woman on
his lap and wondering what to do about her. Having seen
her origins, how she looked without her human veneer,
his insistent desire for her no longer made sense.

Something new: he felt compassion for Dance. She had
witnessed the destruction of her world and her race. With
no concept at all of where she might end up, Dance had
flung herself into the vast domain of space—and ended up
on Matthew Lawton's lap.

"Well?" she said. "What now?"

"If I can help you, I will," said Matthew.

CHAPTER 16

When Matthew regained consciousness, he was being rolled through the Icecube lounge. Drug dispensers were plugged into his arms and chest, and the anxious face of Len Rackham hovered over him.

"Matt, what'd they do to you?" he said.

A feeble gurgle was all the sound Matthew could manage to make. Then a rush of Sting reached his brain and the cobwebs sizzled away. He tried to sit up. The effort blotted his vision with glaring white suns and sent agonizing pain through his limbs.

"Stay flat," warned Len. "You nearly got cooked this time."

"My ship . . . how's the *Bedouin*?"

"We dropped what's left of it on Darkside three hours ago."

"What! Why?"

"The damn thing's hot, Matt. There are enough rads coming off that hull to melt this station to slag. Even if we could decontaminate it, there's not much left of the exostructure. It's all burnt up," said Len.

Matthew lapsed into tormented silence. He had found the Gift, or at least part of it. Of that he was sure. The cost had been high: *Bedouin* ruined; and God knew what would happen to him after bathing in so much hard radiation. Glimpses of Rainbow's cancerous body loomed larger in his memory.

The medics washed him in anti-R fluid. They pumped his stomach and administered an enema. He was injected with Steral and Helidase and half a dozen other drugs. Funny thing was, aside from great fatigue and deep muscular soreness, Matthew was in perfect condition. His skin wasn't blistered or peeling, his hair didn't start falling out, and his gums never bled. In short, he had none of the classic symptoms of radiation poisoning.

In two days he was on his feet again. His fellow dippers, who had formerly regarded him with respect, now looked on him with awe. Matthew seemed indestructible.

Officially, he logged his accident as the result of convection currents hurling his ship into a large spicule. No one asked any questions, though it was common knowledge spicules were not radioactive.

Four days after being found, Matthew borrowed a pogo to visit Darkside Mercury. He wanted to examine the hulk of the *Bedouin*. Arne Dawlish agreed to fly him, but steadfastly refused to go near the hot remains of Matthew's ship.

The pogo *Icecube 9* tracked slowly over the crash zone where the *Bedouin* had been dropped. A number of old ships had been dumped in this area, and it took some time to sort through them. At last, rad-detectors on the pogo chattered volubly.

"I think we found him," said Arne.

"Circle," said Matthew. He flipped the infrared cube

on. Below, the hull of a dipper ship lay cracked open across the lip of a small crater. As the *Icecube 9* turned, Matthew saw the numbers 2-3-1 stencilled on the starboard wingtip.

"That's him. Set down as close as you can," he said.

Arne was appalled. "Close to that?" he piped. "There are enough rads coming out of that hull—"

"Yeah, I know, to melt Icecube to slag. I'm going, Arne, and I don't want to have to walk far in a heavy anti-R suit. So put us down as close as you feel comfortable."

The pogo ghosted over the rim of the crater. Arne applied braking thrust. The landing stilts trailed through the dust a few meters, then settled in the bottom of the crater.

"Not bad," said Matthew, judging the distance. "But it's all uphill."

"Sorry, Matthew," said Arne.

Even in the feeble grip of Mercury's gravity, Matthew's walk across the crater was arduous. The radiation suit was sheathed in metal, and the dust on the crater floor was calf deep. He waded through the silver-gray powder, slinging up showers of particles with every motion of his feet.

The portabeam picked out the scorched hull of the *Bedouin*. Matthew slogged on. His rad-counter nearly went off its scale. Len Rackham was right; the ship was very hot.

The *Bedouin* had hit tail first, and the lightweight metalcomb structure was cracked in a dozen places. Matthew pulled a broken silicon cell from the wreck. It was completely tapped out. There was no flash damage on the hull or the ground, so Matthew knew the cells were empty when it crashed.

The immensely strong pilot module was intact. Matthew threw back the cupola. With the bulky suit on, he couldn't fit in the seat. He leaned in and connected a lead to the audion panel.

"Ahmad, are you there?" he said.

"Yes, sir. May I infer by your presence you are well?" said the audion.

"Well enough. Had a rough trip, eh?"

"Yes, sir. My last, I suspect."

Matthew had a curious reaction to Ahmad's remark. He felt sorry for the doomed machine.

"You were a good copilot, Ahmad. Best I ever had," he said.

"Thank you. I always tried to do my best, sir."

"Is there anything you can tell me about the energy field we encountered?" said Matthew.

"I can only tell you what it was not, sir. It was not atomic, photonic, ionic, or thermal. It exhibited certain characteristics in common with electromagnetic phenomena, but there were sufficient differences as to preclude its being a normal E-M field," said Ahmad.

"I guess if you're going to have an unknown type of energy, the sun's the place for it," said Matthew. "With so much power being generated and expended, strange variations are bound to develop."

"There are flaws in your reasoning, sir, but I will not dispute the fact of our encounter," said the audion. Matthew patted the console with a heavily gloved hand.

"Don't worry, Ahmad. I'll find out what it was," he said.

Before unplugging himself, Matthew heard the audion say: "Sir—Matthew—before you go, would you erase my bubble cards?"

"Sure, Ahmad," he said. He was amused that it had finally used his given name. "Why?" he queried.

"Mercury is a very lonely place," said Ahmad. "It would be better to lose my higher functions than to remain out here alone. It is an unhappy thing to have no one to talk to. Is it strange for me to think this way?"

"Not at all," said Matthew. He pried the access panel off the side of the console. The audion filaments coursed with laser light, and the translucent memory cards shimmered with a million-million bubbles, each a fragment of Ahmad's intelligence.

"So long, Ahmad," he said. He ripped the filaments free and the cards went dark.

Matthew needed a new ship. *Bedouin* had been good in its day, but technical advances had rendered it obsolescent in a mere two years. To get the latest state-of-the-art sundipper, Matthew returned to Earth. He'd seen some of the younger dippers flying craft made by Triangle Photech, a company whose major product line was laser-based technotronics. As an offshoot of their laser work, Photech began making larger, more efficient energy-collecting cells for sundippers. Later, as a prestige-enhancing project for the corporation, they went into ship design and construction.

It was Matthew's good fortune that Photech's headquarters was in the Triangle, a scientific manufacturing zone in the Atlantic District of the Western Hemisphere. Only a few hundred kilometers west of the Triangle was Buncombe Horse Range Ridge, where Matthew had his house.

He pogoed down from Earth orbit to Lenoir, the town where the central service for audion houses in the Black Mountains was located. Matthew arranged for a visit to Photech's plant to see their latest dipper designs. The company was only too happy to oblige; Matthew's trade was eagerly sought, as he was the most famous sundipper extant.

The Triangle didn't resemble a manufacturing center

from the air. Corporate buildings jutted through a heavy canopy of trees, but all the heavy work was done underground. As Matthew's skimmer flew lazily over the area, he noted building styles ranging from the most modern glasstone sine-towers to boxy brick structures dating back to the Age of Impatience.

Photech was one of the modern edifices. Matthew set the skimmer down on a high platform supported by two gracefully intertwined glasstone pillars no thicker than his wrist. An enclosed elevator stood waiting. Two people, a man and a woman, were in it.

The air calmed after the repulsor units shut down. The Photech people emerged from the elevator car and approached the skimmer.

The man put out his hand. "Pro Lawton? I'm Louis McDermott, Coordinator of the Space Products Division." Matthew shook McDermott's doughy hand and turned to his colleague.

"Sian Donnelly," she said, keeping her hands at her sides. "Photech Public Relations."

Sian and Matthew exchanged probing glances. He saw a tall woman, athletic and trim, with dark blonde hair and sea-blue eyes. She saw a lean, swarthy man with cropped white hair, a lined, serious face, and large hands.

"We're very pleased you chose Photech Corporation," said McDermott, breaking in. "You're by far our most famous customer."

"I'm not a customer yet."

"Once you've seen our new Aztec model, I'm sure you will be," said McDermott. With a sweep of his arm, he indicated Matthew should precede him to the lift.

On the way down he continued to study Sian. McDermott rattled on enthusiastically, but Matthew scarcely heard a word he said. Sian, for her part, appraised Matthew right back.

"—and we guarantee an increase in absorption of at least sixty percent, with no concurrent build-up in static load," said McDermott.

"Oh?" said Matthew while looking at Sian. "Is it that good?"

Sian replied, "It's better than you imagine." McDermott continued describing the Aztec.

The elevator stopped at ground level. The three passengers strolled along a crushed stone path toward a low oval dome one hundred meters away.

"How do you like the grounds?" said Sian.

"Very nice," said Matthew. "I've never seen so many trees."

"You're from Luna, aren't you? Not many trees up there," said McDermott.

"I was born on Earth, but lived on Luna most of my life. My official residence now is Icecube Space Station."

"Sounds lonely," said Sian.

"It's not. Sixty people live and work out of Icecube, and it's not a big place," Matthew said. "I'll tell you what is lonely: my house in the mountains. No one lives within thirty km of the place."

"You must like peace and quiet," said Sian.

"Well, quiet anyway."

McDermott punched a code sequence into the lock on the dome entrance. The door slid down. He said, "After you, Mr. Lawton."

Matthew descended a long, sloping ramp. At the bottom, he paused by another codelocked door. It yielded to McDermott's key, and Matthew found himself in a large, brightly lit hangar.

The Aztec filled the room. It was a perfect convex disc, 125 meters in diameter. The edges on either side of the long pilot module curved down. Pedestals supported the craft off the floor.

Matthew ran a hand over the cold, smooth surface of

the ship. "What's this made of?" he said. "It doesn't feel like metal."

"It isn't," McDermott said. "The skin is a silicon-based resin fused to an underlying matrix of graphite and tantalum carbide wire." He smiled. "Lean on her, Pro. See how light she is!"

Matthew pushed down on the ship with his forearms. The big disc tipped easily on its pedestals.

"The entire shell weighs only twelve thousand five hundred kg," said McDermott. "Of course, it will weigh more once engines, instruments, and storage apparatus have been installed."

"What about the collection array? That's what interests me most." McDermott led Matthew and Sian to the center section, which was two meters off the floor. The underside of the Aztec was studded with clear hexagonal cells, over two thousand of them.

"Each cap is one hundred percent Polyclear, the most transparent heat-resistant substance we have. Inside each cell, three Photech selenium capsules convert light, heat, and gravity to spheroidal plasma. Behind the capsules is a two-way Tesla chip, which draws the plasma into a mega-gauss M-bottle," McDermott recited. He walked to the rear of the ship. "On either side of the pilot's compartment are the storage banks."

"What's the maximum capacity?" asked Matthew.

"At one hundred percent load, fifty billion mega-watts." This was three times the *Bedouin*'s capacity.

"The module seems rather big. Is there a Kappa-series audion built in?" said Matthew.

"Yes, and a tandem seat for the copilot," said McDermott.

"I won't need that."

"It's standard equipment," Sian said.

The Aztec was an impressive piece of hardware. It would undoubtedly prove awkward to handle because of its size, but the benefit of a fifty-bmW capacity was worth wrestling with.

"How much?" said Matthew.

"If you mean the price," said Sian, "for you, it'll be zero."

"Zero? Who do I have to kill?"

McDermott laughed insincerely. "No, my Pro, you don't understand. It would be a great boost for Photech if you used our ship. All we ask is that you do some promotional holoids for us."

"Commercials?" said Matthew.

"Advertising," said Sian. McDermott waved his hands about and began talking faster.

"We have a large campaign mapped out. We plan to use the Aztec as a promo feature leading off the rest of our product line," he said. "The first holoid will be very simple. It shows you, in your dipper gear, standing in front of this ship. You look right at the camera and say, 'Aztec—cuts the heart out of the sun.'" Behind McDermott's back, Sian gave a grimace of disgust.

Matthew folded his fingers together and sighed. "How much would the Aztec cost if you were to sell it?"

McDermott thought for a moment, then said, "Well, engine included and audion installed, the cost would be, say, one hundred fifty megalots. Add a forty percent markup for profit and we're talking about two hundred ten megalots."

"I'll pay it," said Matthew. McDermott almost choked, and Sian blinked rapidly in surprise.

"You'll *pay?*" she said.

"It's a lot, but the ship appears worth it," he said. "How soon can you have it finished?"

"But the promotional campaign—" protested McDermott.

"I'm not interested," said Matthew. "Do you want the money now?"

Sian said in oddly measured tones, "You have two hundred ten megalots?"

"I have a lot more than that."

McDermott's face was red. "I'll have to speak to the corporate board; so much was expected from the ads . . . *two hundred ten megalots!*"

"Cash, if you like." Matthew couldn't resist tormenting them. He had long since stopped caring about the size of his bank account, but he always was amused by other people's reactions when he dropped large figures on their heads.

"I need the ship as soon as possible," he said. "When can it be ready?"

"Ready? For you, my Pro, ten days. No, seven!" said McDermott.

"Good. I'll stay in the Triangle till it's done." He said to Sian, "Where's a good place to stay around here?"

"The Hotel Raleigh is the best we have," she said. She scribbled the address on a pressure pad and gave it to him. "I'll call ahead for you and reserve a suite."

"Just a room will do," said Matthew. "I wouldn't know what to do in a suite." McDermott thought this was a joke and laughed. When Sian and Matthew didn't, he reddened and fell silent.

Back at Matthew's skimmer, McDermott pumped his hand vigorously until Matthew snatched it away. He offered his hand to Sian.

"I hope to see you again, Ms. Donnelly," he said.

"Sian," she said. "I'm certain you will."

It wasn't until he was aloft that Matthew noticed what was written at the bottom of the pad Sian had given him. It was another address and a telaudion connection code.

The Raleigh was furnished in what Matthew thought of as "Concordat Chic," meaning little features were included in the decor to cater to nonterrestrial guests. Belly pads for Anubans. Scintillators for Freyans. High humidity settings for the amphibious natives of Perun. Matthew wondered if the hotel had ever had any alien visitors, or included the frills to impress its provincial guests.

The room was clean and comfortable and the rates tolerable. Matthew ate in his room that evening, facing the wide plexi windows. As the sun set, lights went on all over the Triangle. It was amusing to see how small cities still believed many lights made them urbane, while large metropolitan centers struggled to darken their garish environs.

At 21:00 Matthew went to the telaudion and asked for Sian's home. He got a voice link only.

"Yes?"

"This is Matthew Lawton." The cube came on. Sian was smiling.

"How are you, Mr. Lawton?" she said.

"Bored. Lonely. I thought you might give me some more advice, seeing as your hotel tip turned out well," he said.

"What sort of advice, Mr. Lawton?"

"What do people around here do for fun?"

"The usual things."

"I'm a sundipper. I can't do my usual things on Earth," he said.

"Hmm, that's true," said Sian. "Do you like Novex?" This was a popular "happy" drug.

"I prefer *E*-vodka, or rum-and-bay."

"What a coincidence; I have two liters of each on hand. I seldom drink either myself, but I do like to keep some on hand for my friends."

"Am I a friend, Sian?"

"I don't know yet. Why don't you come over and we'll discuss it."

Sian lived in Orange, the western end of the Triangle. Her neighborhood was consciously quaint and trendy, which tended to confirm the ideas Matthew was already forming.

Sian was aggressive, attractive, and ambitious. She was also curious about the dippers' legendary Gift. Matthew was amenable to helping her find out the truth. He had his own reasons. He'd been alone since Gem disappeared (almost three quarters), and the need was there. He also wondered how his close contact with the strange energy field had affected him.

He identified himself to the building audion and went up. Sian answered the door in person.

"Come in, Matthew. Or is it Matt?" she said.

"I answer to both," he said. He followed her into the apartment.

Her apparel was provocative and annoying. Sian wore a vacuum suit, a garment made from two sheets of perforated vinyl, applied with suction until it fitted skin-tight. Sian's was wine red, and left nothing to his imagination. She might as well have worn a coat of paint.

The apartment was in the popular style. Matthew sank into a gelchair and accepted a heavy tumbler of *E*-vodka. The first sign of individuality he detected was in her choice of music. Skywave would've been usual for a woman of Sian's age and inclinations; instead her musicon was playing Beethoven's Fifth Piano Concerto.

"Don't you have any friends on Earth?" said Sian, curling up in another gelchair.

"Not anymore," he replied. "I haven't lived onworld since I was seven. My colleagues are my friends now."

"That's funny. I can't imagine being close to the people you compete with," she said.

"Working dippers don't compete with each other," said Matthew. "There's plenty of sun for everybody."

They chatted like this for hours, and Matthew gradually lost his mildly contemptuous feeling for Sian. Some of his earlier notions proved correct. She was very ambitious.

She described her maneuverings to oust her boss, Pro Dodgson, in cold, clinical detail. Then a different spirit would seize her, and she would rhapsodize on the genius of Beethoven, or speak wistfully of visiting the inhabited planets of the Concordat. There were subtleties to Sian he would never have suspected. Matthew began to like her.

It grew late. They parted with an amiable kiss, like old friends. Matthew felt good being proved wrong in his deductions. It didn't happen often.

CHAPTER 17

Four notes chimed in the still house. A pause, and the notes sounded again. The house said, "Mr. Lawton, there is a telaudion call for you."

Matthew rubbed his face. His right eye was red and swollen from Dance's use, and he'd taken an analgesic to relieve the irritation. It worked so well he fell asleep on the living room couch.

"Who is it?" he said loudly. The chronograph showed 1:37.

"The linker has not given a name, but it originates from the neighboring dwelling," said the house.

He reached across the low arm of the couch and tapped the telaudion panel. Dance appeared.

"Matthew, did you just try to call me?" she said.

"Huh? No, I didn't. I was dozing."

"Someone did, and it was very disturbing. Each terminal in the house came on in succession, and there was no answer when I spoke. All there was was a low-volume, high-pitched beeping."

His drowsiness vanished. "Dance, you've got to get out of there immediately. The police are coming."

"How do you know?"

"West Hemi constables carry audion sweepers, which let them scan inside computerized houses. They probed your place to make sure you're there. They're on their way. Get out, now!"

She hesitated. "Where can I go? I sent David's skimmer and chauffeur away and told them not to come back."

"Come over here. I'll hide you."

"They will search your house once they find I am gone."

"They won't get past me," he vowed.

"I will come," said Dance. She turned away from the cube for a second. "May I bring my elpees? I would dislike leaving them behind."

"No, Dance. It must look like you fled hastily. We don't want them over here in force, which might happen if they think you moved in with me."

She agreed and broke the link. Fifteen minutes later, Dance struggled up the ladder to Matthew's porch. A far-off swishing sound caught her ear. She looked south. Two vehicles were coming.

"Get in!" said Matthew, tugging her sharply through the plexi door. "Go to the revival room and lock the door. Don't open it for anyone."

"Even you?"

"I know the code. Go on!"

The two skimmers separated. One rushed in fast and skidded to a halt on Dance's roof. The other stayed aloft and hovered midway between the two houses.

Matthew went to his bedroom, which faced Dance's house. With a light-enhancing opticon, he watched two men leave the landed skimmer. They were not in uniform. Their vehicle was unmarked.

Matthew was surprised. The Continental Constabulary were always uniformed in conspicuous red jumpsuits. The two intruders wore dark civilian clothes. He focused on the hovering skimmer and saw it too was unmarked. Who were these people?

The telaudion cube at Matthew's bedside began to hum. They were scanning his house now. He went to the cube and opened the link.

"Who is it?" he said casually. The open band remained quiet, though he knew they could hear him. "Who's there?" he said. The link ended.

"Come on down, you bastards," Matthew whispered to himself. He slipped the plasmer into his overshirt pocket.

A soft, scraping noise overhead warned him the second skimmer had landed. The occupants would have no trouble gaining access through the roof hatch. Matthew went down to the living room, set a chair facing the bottom of the stairs, and waited in the dark with gun in hand for his unwelcome visitors.

He heard a *tick-tick-tick*. A man's feet appeared in the spiral loop of steps. He held an infrared ghost detector, which revealed the fading trail of heat Matthew left everywhere he walked or sat. The second man carried a stunning rod.

Matthew hit the lights. The men froze.

"The last thing I thought I'd have to worry about on a mountaintop was burglars," said Matthew, aiming his plasmer at the leading man.

"Just a minute, friend. We aren't burglars," said the rod carrier.

"I don't know you, and you're in my house uninvited. What else should I call you?" said Matthew.

"We're here on official business," said the rod carrier.

"Police?"

"Not exactly."

Matthew adjusted the plasmer for rapid fire. "Then I'll burn you both and toss your bodies down the mountain-side," he said.

"No, wait," said the detector user. "We're not the constabulary, but we do represent the government."

"What government?"

The two men exchanged glances. "The World Benefi-cial Party," said the rod man.

"Not my government," said Matthew. "I'm a free spacer."

"We know. You're Matthew Lawton, the sundipper. Believe me, Pro Lawton, we wouldn't be here if it weren't a matter of global importance," said the man with the detector.

"Explain."

"A very dangerous criminal—a murderer—is in the area. We believe she was living in the house next to yours," said Rod Man.

"You mean Sasha Mackensen?" said Matthew. Anoth-er significant look passed between the men.

Detector Man said, "Mrs. Mackensen is wanted for questioning in the death of her husband, Atlantic District Party Chairman David Mackensen."

"He called it murder," said Matthew, waving the plasmer tip at Rod Man. "If it was, why didn't the police come for her instead of you guys?"

"The Party likes to handle its own problems, my Pro," said Detector Man. "It's our intention to hand Mrs. Mackensen over to the constabulary as soon as we find her."

"You're lying. You want her for some reason of your own."

Detector Man moved down from the stairs and took a half step toward Matthew. "If you know where she is, I advise you to tell us," he said.

Matthew jumped to his feet. "It's none of your damn business! So call the constables or get the hell out!"

Rod Man regarded the plasmer. "That weapon is illegal on Earth," he said. "You could be arrested for possessing it."

"I think I will burn you. I can set your skimmer to crash, and who'll know the difference between plasmer burns and a flash fire?" said Matthew. Rod Man backed up a step.

"You know, Cliff, I think Pro Lawton knows more about Mrs. Mackensen than he's admitting. I think she's right here, in this house. Maybe in his bed," he said. His snide comment stung Matthew to a hasty act. He straightened his arm and fired. The bolt sizzled past Detector Man's thigh. He gave a harsh cry of pain and collapsed, clutching his leg. The plasma just grazed his flesh, leaving a smoking ten-cm burn before expending its energy on the glasstone wall beyond.

"Holy shit!" said Rod Man. He clattered down to his companion and hauled him to his feet. "You must be fucking crazy!"

"I'm a sundipper, remember? We're all fucking crazy," Matthew said. He was shaking inside, but he kept his hand steady and his voice low. "Get out of here and don't come back."

"We'll find her," Rod Man said. "We'll find her and we'll get her!" The BP men struggled up the stairs. A minute later Matthew saw their skimmer swoop down the mountainside at high speed.

Matthew threw the gun across the room. He'd never shot anyone in his life, and it sickened him to realize he would have killed both men with no more provocation than a single smutty remark.

He decoded the door of the revival room. Dance was crouching beneath the plexi "coffin."

"You can come out, they're gone," he said. She stood but was visibly trembling. "It's all right. I got rid of them."

"There was a terrible discharge," said Dance. "I nearly fainted from it. What happened?"

He gathered her into his arms. "Nothing to worry about. I fired the plasmer to scare them. I forgot you'd feel it too," he said.

"Who were they?"

"Agents of the Party. Pro Taylor really wants to get her hands on you."

"What shall I do?"

"Clear out. Off-world would be best—Mars, Luna, the Sky Islands. The Concordat strictly limits the activities of the BP away from Earth." He ran his fingers through the smooth skein of her hair.

"Will you help me escape?"

Matthew dropped his enveloping arms and remembered to whom and to what he was speaking.

"I'll fly you out myself," he said.

Dance watched quietly as Matthew packed. He had said nothing for a long time.

"What distracts you?" she asked.

He paused. "Your appearance. Can you change it?"

"Not without great difficulty and a long interval of isolation. This human veneer I wear is not a garment, Matthew. I cannot change it overnight. The techniques I learned from the hHoma alter the outer skin surfaces according to whatever genetic code I used. My hair and features are living tissue. I cannot shed them when I wish. Why do you want me to? Am I not less conspicuous as a human?"

"Yes, but I'm thinking of how difficult the Party can make things if they try. They'll watch my pogo at Cape Canaveral, and all commercial orbital flights for you," he said. He pressed the zipseams of his travel bag together. "And," he said in a much lower voice, "I keep forgetting what you are. It's frustrating being around you knowing we can't . . . be closer than we are now."

"I have never understood this sexual drive," said Dance. "How do beings attain a high civilization when their bodies obsess them so? I think our way is better, leaving reproduction behind before adulthood comes."

Matthew refused to debate the matter. He switched to another delicate topic.

"Dance, how often do you feed? I was wondering, you see, since it's been several days since Cass Brooks was here," he said.

"It is true I am hungry. Usually, the frequency of my feeding depends on the rate at which I expend energy. Before Cass I was desperate. From the time David died until the night of your party I did not feed."

He said, "When you tried to break into the laser cable, was that just crazed hunger, or can you actually assimilate different forms of energy?"

Dance wrinkled her nose in a purely human way. "I was, as you say, unthinking from hunger. I cannot utilize coherent light. I must have biological energy," she said. "What is more, human energy has become so appealing to me, it would be hard to accept anything else."

"Too bad. I thought you might learn to develop a taste for artificial sources. If we travel together, things may get tough for you. It'll be dangerous for you to find, ah, donors, as long as we're trying to keep a low profile," he said. "I'd help you myself, but I guess I wouldn't taste very good."

"I appreciate the offer, Matthew."

He slung one bag over his shoulder and tucked the

other under his arm. "I'll call Lenoir. My skimmer will be
here in half an hour."

"Where are we going?" asked Dance.

"Albemarle Depot," he said.

CHAPTER 18

Matthew haunted the premises of Triangle Photech for a week, popping in at odd hours to inspect the progress on his new ship. He decided he liked the model name, and thereafter referred to it as the *Aztec*. Louis McDermott always insisted on being on hand to escort Matthew, and almost had a nervous breakdown. Two hundred and ten megalots bought a lot of service at Photech.

Work on the *Aztec* proceeded, and Matthew found his interest turning more and more toward Sian Donnelly. Since his initial visit, he'd made a point of asking for her, and soon McDermott never showed up without her. Sian, less awed by Matthew's wealth, displayed tolerant amusement each time McDermott dragged her from her office with the words: "Pro Lawton is here!"

Matthew and Sian dined together in Orange twice. The restaurants were small and dark, the food overpriced and mediocre, but Matthew enjoyed himself immensely. Sian took nothing for granted. She was a constant challenge, so much so he felt he was always on trial—all right, Lawton, what makes you so damn good?

These feelings of interest and excitement misled him. By the end of the week Matthew believed he was in love with Sian Donnelly.

They had dinner for the third time at the Hotel Raleigh. During the salad course, Sian played her cards.

"How do you feel about the Great Outdoors?" she said.

"Neutral. I've never been exposed to it," he said.

"Would you like to be? Visit the country, I mean."

He looked at her blankly. She said, "I have a cabin about a hundred km northeast of here. It's very remote, on the shore of a large lake. How'd you like to spend a few days there?"

"With you?"

"Well of course, dummy. There'd be no point in going alone."

Matthew smiled and raised his glass. "I accept," he said.

The flight to the lake was one Matthew would long remember. Sian flew without a stabilizer; consequently the vehicle dipped, soared, and wobbled like a leaf in an autumn whirlwind. Matthew held tightly to his seat brace and grunted monosyllabic replies to Sian's carefree comments.

By contemporary standards Sian's retreat was primitive. There wasn't even a telaudion in the three-room cabin. No holoid cube, no microwave oven—just an old-fashioned gas stove and a powerful Nansuto musicon.

"Some place," said Matthew, dumping his bags on the floor. Sian went to the enormous couch and pulled off the cushions.

"This folds out into a bed," she said. "You'll be comfortable here."

Matthew could see a full-size bed in the next room. "Is that yours?"

"All mine," said Sian, deadpan.

Matthew pursed his lips and said nothing.

They stowed the food they had brought. By the time they were done the sun was setting. Sian peeked out the kitchen window and said, "Oh! Let's go down to the dock. Sunsets are wonderful on the water."

She led him down a narrow path to the lake's edge. A short pier jutted out into the lake. Beside it was a ramshackle boathouse.

Sian went briskly to the end of the pier. Matthew followed more slowly. The sun, magnified by layers of air and dust, seemed twice normal size and candy-apple red. Where its ruddy glow fell on the water, the lake glowed with distant stellar fire.

Sian shoved her hands into her pockets and stared at the sun. Matthew stopped by her side.

"Beautiful, isn't it?" she said.

"Hmm, yes," he said, thinking of her and not the view.

"What's it like to touch the sun?"

"Hot. Very, very hot."

"Seriously."

He put an arm across Sian's back and let his hand rest on her hip. "Seriously, it's the most exciting thing a person can do," he said.

"*Most* exciting?"

"Nothing else comes close."

"I wish I could go sometime," she said.

"Dippers don't take passengers."

"They say it changes you. They say dippers are paid millions, but most of them would do it for nothing."

"That's true. Money loses significance when you've felt all that power grip you," he said.

"And once your bank account goes past five hundred megalots, it's hardly worth counting, is it?" she replied.

He glanced at Sian suspiciously. By the dying diurnal light her profile resembled a fine copper statue.

"Let's go back to the house and make love," he said.

Sian laughed, her happy mockery echoing across the calm surface of the lake. "My, aren't we blunt!" she said. "Is that your usual line, or are you being extra smooth for my sake?"

Matthew was abashed. He hadn't made such a clumsy overture in years.

"Just thinking out loud," he said gruffly.

"Never mind," said Sian, linking her arm in his. "I'm starved. I'll cook tonight. Have you ever heard of Donnelly's famous Irish spaghetti?"

"No. What makes it Irish?"

"The cook," she said. "Only the cook."

He slept badly on the couch and awoke stiff. Sian was breezing about the tiny kitchen, making an ungodly racket with pots and pans. She called a cheery greeting to Matthew as the latter stumped to the bathroom. He was appalled to find a water-flush toilet and a sink and tub served by faucets. The fixtures were museum pieces.

"How old is this house?" Matthew asked as he sat down at the kitchen table.

"I really don't know," said Sian. "I think it was built fifty years before the First Concordat."

"It's very well preserved."

"Old-timers built things to last."

After breakfast they went to the boathouse. Inside was a four-meter fiberglass centerboard sloop, with the mast unstepped. The name on the transom read *Amigo*.

"Do you sail?" said Sian.

"No."

"Want to?"

A cold sensation settled in the pit of Matthew's stomach, right next to Sian's bacon omelet. "I'd rather not," he said.

"Oh, why?"

"Looks dangerous." Sian dissolved in a fit of laughter. "What's so damned hysterical?" demanded Matthew.

"You," she gasped. "A man who flies through the worst inferno in space, afraid of a sailboat!"

"Can you handle it?" he said, bristling. Sian nodded, voiceless with mirth. "OK, Sinbad, let's go!"

They poled the *Amigo* from the boathouse and looped a painter line from the bow to a cleat on the shed. Sian said, "We have to raise the mast."

The mast was a formidable pole, six meters of aluminum and steel. Matthew braced his feet apart and pushed his hands slowly up the pole as Sian fed a line from the peak to a hand winch at the bow. As the tension increased Matthew had less and less grip on the heavy pole. With only his fingertips to control it, he stretched his arms higher and higher. He leaned too far left. The boat tipped.

"Easy!" said Sian.

Matthew tried to correct the list by shifting his weight right. *Amigo* rocked to starboard. Sian clapped a hand in the scupper and held on. Matthew grabbed onto the nearest thing at hand: the mast. The mast swung on its pivot first right, then left, until Matthew toppled over the side back first into the water.

Sian giggled. She held a hand to her mouth to stifle her amusement. Matthew erupted from the three-meter-deep water, sputtering and hacking.

"Help me!" he cried.

Sian jumped in feet first and reached him in two short strokes. "Take it easy, Matt. I've got you," she said. It wasn't that simple. Matthew wrapped a panic-strong arm around her and dragged Sian down with him. She struggled to free herself, but he clutched desperately at her shirt with his other hand.

They heaved up for air. "Damn it, let go!" Sian gasped. Down they went again. Sian was no match for Matthew in strength, but she had no intention of drowning three meters from a dock. She drove a fist into his belly. Matthew's remaining air whooshed out, and he let go. She hooked an arm around his neck and towed him through the open door of the boathouse. Sian deposited him unresisting on the slimy wooden steps below the pier.

"Why didn't you say you couldn't swim?" panted Sian.

"Tired of—being—laughed at." Matthew hugged a piling and coughed the liquid from his lungs. She helped him sit up on the dock. A few breaths later he said, "Living on Luna and in space doesn't expose you to many swimming pools." Sian wearily agreed.

A bumping sound took her attention away. The sailboat was bobbing in the wind and wearing against the end of the pier. She walked, sodden, to the near set of cleats and secured the stern.

Coming back, she saw Matthew lying limply on his side, facing away. "Matt?" she said. "Matt, are you all right?" He didn't answer. Sian rushed to him and knelt beside his unmoving form.

"Ha!" he shouted, twisting quickly on his back and grabbing Sian by the arms. He pulled her down and kissed her. He tasted lake water and black coffee and felt her struggle. Matthew let go. Sian fell back.

"You bastard," she said. "Do you know how much you scared me?"

"Which time? Faking the faint or kissing you?"

"Both."

He brushed a line of damp ringlets away from her cheek and kissed her again. This time there was no struggle of resistance, only of cooperation. Their wet clothing was devilishly hard to shed, but they eventually got rid of it all. Sian and Matthew made love on the water-worn boards twice and again. The old shed resounded with their cries.

Sian dangled her feet in the cold, muddy lake. Matthew, flat on his back behind her, watched as beads of water dripped from her hair and rolled with increasing speed down either side of her supple spine.

"Question," he said.

"Hmm?"

"Why did we wait so long?"

"What d'you mean?"

"What we did was good, wasn't it?"

"Yes, very."

"We could have begun a long time ago," he said.

"I didn't want to till two hours ago," said Sian simply.

"I thought we clicked right off, the first day I came to Photech."

"We did. You're very attractive, Matt, but I have standards. I don't waste myself on selfish, arrogant men. The first few times we were together, I got the feeling you thought all you had to do was snap your brown fingers and my clothes would automatically fall to my feet."

She had him pegged. He'd traded on the reputation of the sundippers to the point he felt only contempt for his bed partners. Now, after two splendid hours, he was strangely desirous of praise. He asked quite diffidently if Sian had enjoyed herself.

"No," she said calmly. "It wasn't fun. It was more. . . significant, if I may use that word. The stories about dippers are true, aren't they?" He admitted they were. "You have some cause to be arrogant, then. But you'd best remember, this gift of yours is an accident. You weren't born with it, my friend."

Another droplet rippled along the nubs of her backbone. Matthew stopped it with his tongue. Sian shuddered.

"I don't know if I'm going to love you or hate you," she said. "Either way, it's going to be an experience." She turned to face him, but before he could bring her close, she put a hand to his chest. "Which will it be?"

A shadow flashed across Matthew's face. A day earlier, he would have been certain of his answer.

"I don't know," he said truthfully. Sian removed her hand.

CHAPTER 19

The Ontario Dynamics skimmer settled precisely on Matthew's roof. He had to admire the skill of a pilot who could set a vehicle down so exactly in a fierce crosswind. Gusts across the rooftop were so strong Dance clung to his arm just to keep her footing.

The skimmer door rolled back. The pilot's seat was empty.

Matthew flung his belongings into the rear, then helped Dance in the passenger side. He slid into the pilot's seat and said, "Nice landing, Leonardo."

"Thank you, sir," said the audion. "Conditions were most trying."

"Is it common to have an audion in so small a vehicle?" asked Dance.

"They all have some degree of computer stabilization," Matthew said as he keyed the repulsors. "I had Leonardo specially installed. It's quite an advantage. It could navigate this car to Shiva, couldn't you?"

"Easily, sir."

"Why do you call it Leonardo?" she said.

"I am named after the Italian artist Leonardo da Vinci, 596 to 529 P.C.," said the audion.

"P.C.?" said Dance.

"Pre-Concordat," said Matthew and Leonardo together. Matthew gripped the Z-shaped flight stick in his right hand and rested his left on the trackball speed control. "Here we go," he said.

The skimmer rose ten meters and swung right. They drifted over Dance's house on the "downhill" impetus of the lifting repulsors. Once they were centered, Matthew touched down on her roof. Dance went to fetch her meager possessions. She returned with the precious elpees and the player.

Matthew put the skimmer into a steep climb. The rearview cube showed their houses shrinking in the distance. It was an emotional moment for him. Depending on circumstances, he might never return to Buncombe Horse Range Ridge. He thought of Sian and her silent departure from his life. There had been nothing to say. Sian, like the house, proved expendable.

"Course perturbation," warned Leonardo. Matthew snapped back to reality. He corrected the skimmer's attitude and stroked the trackball for more speed. At 8,200 meters there was little to fear from collision. He laid in the course for Albemarle Depot and let Leonardo take over. The skimmer flew smoothly on.

Matthew didn't relax. He was thinking hard about an idea that had come to him the night before.

If Dance were to survive, she (it! why couldn't he remember *it?*) would have to have a safe and reliable source of nourishment. Approaching strange men was too chancy. Paying for her meals seemed unfeasible (how much were they worth?).

Was there a synthetic substitute for human life-energy? Dance had tried to tap a laser line . . . coherent light . . .

There was the Gift.

"Dance?" he said.

"Yes, Matthew?"

"I've an idea of how you can escape Taylor and live well in the bargain."

"How is that, Matthew?"

"Sundipping." He explained how free spacers were not under any authority save the Concordat's; how much money could be made dipping, and how the guild of dippers protected each other from outsiders. Then Matthew revealed his *coup de main*.

"This thing that prevents you from feeding on me, what I call the Gift? Working in the sun will put the Gift into you, Dance. If my theory's correct, every dip you make will be a banquet. The sun generates life for the entire solar system, and you'll be able to tap it at the source," he said.

"Suppose I cannot assimilate the energy?" replied Dance. "I would find myself in a colony of humans like yourself, whose life-energy would be unusable to me. I would starve to death, Matthew. In the midst of a station full of beings, in the glare of life itself, I would starve to death."

"What choice have you got?" asked Matthew. "Roam Luna, preying on unwary factory workers? Or Mars, among the sandfoot farmers? I'll bet they taste real good!"

"You don't know the need, Matthew, the emptiness. I had no conception of hunger before the hHoma came. Since those terrible sleeps in space, I have lived in fear of my hunger. It is the worst thing, Matthew, and I will do anything to avoid it."

"I'm offering you a chance to never be hungry again."

"Your offer is kind, but I think it stems from an

impossible concept of companionship. I cannot stay with you if it means my death."

Matthew pushed back his seat and rotated around to Dance. He tugged his shirt open at the collar.

"We'll find out right now if you can tolerate the Gift," he said harshly.

"You know I cannot."

"Bullshit. Humans eat things that're harsh and dangerous. Let's see what you can stomach," he said. Matthew seized her left hand and dragged it to his chest.

"No, please!" Dance protested. She was far too frail to escape his grip. He placed her fingers over his heart. She struggled feebly. Her resistance excited him. Matthew pulled Dance out of her seat and clamped a hand on her other wrist.

Her right hand brushed his sternum. When the fingers made good contact with the skin over his solar plexus, tingling currents began to spread in concentric circles outward from the nerve center. The sensation crept upward through the trunk of his body. His heart pumped arhythmically for a few seconds, then adjusted to a new cycle—Dance's.

The feedback from Dance's draining crawled up Matthew's neck. He imagined it as a snake, formed of white-hot plasma, seeking entry into his brain. It found its way, and his head opened outward like a blossoming rose.

Dance heaved back, making strangled hissing sounds. No matter how she lunged, he wouldn't let go. She shook so violently that the audion increased its stabilization by three marks, the equivalent of flying through a major storm.

Matthew's vision cleared enough for him to see Dance's face. As when she'd been with Brooks, her human eyeshells had now been forced out by the pressure of her true eyes expanding. The bone-white orbs were streaked with blue; as he watched they gradually changed to black.

"I am sated," Dance whimpered. "Release me, please, Matthew." He did. Breaking contact disrupted his heartbeat again. He stiffened in agony as his body tried to regain control of itself. Dance collapsed in her seat.

The thudding in his ears faded. Matthew wiped the sweat from his face and said, "I didn't know it'd be so severe."

Dance carefully replaced her eyeshells. "You are a severe man," she said. "But I detect some benefit in your severity. Under gentler circumstances, I may be able to consume this sun energy. But not from you. Your responses are too harsh. They cause pain."

Matthew knew the pain. He knew it, yet somehow it gave him pleasure.

He straightened his seat and kept his gaze focused beyond the windscreen. The trip aerometer showed 620 kilometers to go.

Mountains subsided into hills, and the hills declined into heavily wooded plains. Abruptly the forests vanished, to be replaced with wide, open land, dotted with scrub pines and streaked with sand. Creeks and rivers interlaced the coastal plain, all leading down to the sea. Warm, moist haze hung in the air, graying the sky and making visibility difficult.

Matthew began calling Albemarle Depot from seventy-five km out. Depot Air Control was surprised to get a private call, but Matthew mentioned enough money to smooth over any rough spots in their negotiations.

Albemarle Depot was an artificial island, two km in diameter, anchored in Albemarle Sound eleven km south of Wade Point. It served as a base for shipping food products of the Atlantic (such as krill, a staple of the Martian diet) to Earth orbit. Sea hoppers skated in from south and east, and transport pogos lofted their cargoes into space for transferral to waiting ships. Using the island

platform spared the inhabited areas of East Atlantica
from the noise and congestion of a heavily used spaceport.
The Depot was stable, safe, and protected from the open
sea by the Outer Banks.

Matthew landed on the No. 3 east pad. The sun was
bright and the offshore wind cool as he and Dance
disembarked. A woman with a badge reading *Asst. Depot
Mgr.* approached them.

"Are you Lawton?" she said. "Dupree, acting manager. We got your message. Why'd you come to us instead of
one of the passenger ports?"

"It's a long story, Pro Dupree. What it burns down to is
this: certain people want to stop my friend and me from
leaving," said Matthew.

Dupree grinned. "Husband, father, or brother?" she
said. Matthew gave a noncommittal shrug and Dupree
laughed.

"Where'd you want to go?" she said.

"Just to orbit. Once there, we'll take any ship we can
get."

Dupree consulted a memo chip on her wrist. "OK, you
can go as supercargo on the *Neuse*. It'll be taking off in
eighteen minutes. Is this all your baggage?" Dance and
Matthew nodded. "Carry it on yourselves. This ain't the
Emperors' Line, you know."

The *Neuse* was one of the biggest pogos Matthew had
ever seen, easily exceeding eight thousand tons dead-
weight. Its cargo was ten thousand crates of dehydrated
krill. This wasn't the first fish run the *Neuse* had made; the
pogo was filthy, and the interior reeked of ancient sea-
food. Matthew and Dance made their way to the lofty
passenger area, an enclosed plexi box twelve meters long
by three meters wide. They sat down in some hard plastic
chairs and looked down as the handlers crammed the last
crates of krill into the hold.

"Attention: six minutes to lift-off," said a PA speaker. "Six minutes."

"Where are we going?" asked Dance.

"Luna," Matthew said. "To the city where I used to live, Tycho Basin."

"Four minutes," bellowed the PA.

Loud clangs rang below. The huge cargo doors were being shut. All were sealed except the main portside hatch. A knot of men stood in the way. They waved their arms a lot and pointed toward the passenger cabin.

A crewman in gray appeared at the bow end of the cabin. "Lawton, there's some people down there who want you and the woman," he said.

"Throw them out and take off. I'm paying dear for this flight, but you'll never see the money if I don't make it," said Matthew.

The shouting match ended in a flurry of fists. The Party agents (no more than three of them) were pummeled and expelled from the *Neuse*. The last hatch closed.

"Forty seconds to take-off," said the PA.

"Strap yourself in," Matthew warned. "This'll be rough."

Pogo operators don't waste money on niceties like servo-stabilizers or velpad chairs for passengers. The *Neuse* rumbled off Albemarle Depot with the ease of an avalanche. It gained speed in rugged leaps and bounds, slinging the hapless supercargo against their restraints. G forces increased rapidly, then faded. *Neuse* achieved orbit in seven minutes, twelve seconds.

"What a knockabout!" said Matthew. He loosened his straps and drifted free of the seat. No artificial gravity. Typical.

"How did the Party know we would be leaving from Albemarle?" said Dance.

"I don't know; maybe they trailed us. Or maybe they

had agents at every spaceport on the Atlantic coast. Who knows? We're away, and they won't catch us now," he said.

Neuse made four orbits before rendezvousing with its target vessel, the Martian freighter *Johnny Unitas*. The Martian ship was a great boxy craft, consisting of little more than a series of cargo bays, engines, and a control room. The *Neuse* could easily have parked in one of the *Unitas*'s bays.

Shifting cargo was easy in zero G. Handlers hoisted thousand-kilo crates and walked blithely across the transfer tunnel to the *Unitas*.

Dance walked daintily on her toes, keeping her fingertips on the ceiling and pushing down. Matthew followed her to the airlock. A Martian spacer stopped them.

"Who're you?" he said.

"I'm Jekyll and this is Hyde. We need quick passage to Luna, if you're going that way and have the room," said Matthew.

"We've no arrangements for passengers," said the spacer. "No 'menities, nothing."

"Give us room to stand and we will be well," said Dance.

The Martian shrugged. "Same as same," he said. "I'll yakk the purser; you pay her."

Neuse cleared the freighter and plunged back into the atmosphere. The *Unitas* activated its artificial gravity and prepared to leave orbit.

When the spacer said "no 'menities" he wasn't joking. Matthew and Dance wedged themselves among the man-size cartons of biomase, the liquid growth medium used in the bacteria farms on Luna. The *Unitas* moved out slowly for Earth's satellite, using only one engine. It took them two days to get there.

Matthew paid the purser, and he and Dance rode down to Luna in the gig with the First Guide. They landed at Fra

Mauro moonfall. The gig was lowered into a handling pit. As soon as the outer hatch opened, they were inundated by a throng of Lunarians, all shouting at the First Guide for jobs on her outward-bound ship. The mistress of the *Johnny Unitas* swept the gabbling mob aside with a contemptuous glare. They parted as if burned when she and her passengers stepped down, only to engulf the gig's crew when they emerged.

"Are conditions so bad that people lie in wait for every ship that lands here?" asked Dance.

"Things aren't so bad," said the First Guide. "Fifty km away, audion chip factories are crying for workers. This lot are chronic job-jumpers."

Dance looked blank. Matthew explained, "They wander all over Luna, begging for jobs. First time they get paid, they quit and live on their starting wages until it's time to go begging again."

Fra Mauro was a crude place, with cut-stone tunnels and dust-flecked plexi on the surface runs. The First Guide of the *Unitas* parted company with Dance and Matthew at the offices of her parent company, Stay-Aloft, Inc. The latter pair stepped on the midlevel conveyor. This would carry them to the bus terminal.

As they rode Dance noticed the haughty upper-class colonists, or "Selenites" as they preferred to be called. Several generations of living on the moon had affected their physiognomy in a distinctive way. Selenites towered up to two meters in height. Their skin was a rich red brown, not unlike a sundipper's, and their heads and hands were larger than Earth normal. Selenites regarded spacers like Matthew with condescension, but reserved true scorn for the lower classes of their own world, the Dusters.

The tunnel ended. Matthew and Dance emerged from the sublunar settlement into a dazzling, sunlit surface run. Holoid letters glowed overhead, proclaiming *Tranquility,*

2,490 km; Tycho Basin, 1,826 km; Aristarchus via Tycho, 5,478 km.

"Go left," said Matthew. The conveyor ended at a wide platform. The next bus wasn't due for thirty minutes. A queue had formed. Most of the beings in it were Earth folk, returning to Tycho. A sprinkle of aliens were present: half a dozen Freyans, a pair of Anubans, a large green Peruni with scales and spiny hands, and a lone ameboid in its tank. The crowd waited patiently, their murmuring voices filling the platform.

Ten minutes after Matthew and Dance arrived, a piercing shriek ripped the air. Matthew jerked around in time to see a close-moving band of Lunarians come racketing out of the Fra Mauro tunnel.

"Dusters!" someone cried. The line shrank back as twenty young toughs swarmed onto the bus platform. They shoved their way through the crowd, tapping metal rods across the chests of anyone who seemed inclined to resist. The Dusters rapidly isolated their targets, the nonhumans.

"We don't want you here," said a male Duster whose face was stipled with appliques. "You smell bad, you talk worse, and you take jobs away from real people!"

"I'm only a tourist," objected a Freyan mildly.

The appliqued Duster swung his rod in a wide arc that ended against the Freyan's head. The blue-skinned being toppled without a sound. Other onlookers cried out in protest and anger. The vocal Duster raised his rod to an East Hemi woman.

"We don't like Earthers much either," he said. "So stitch it, or you'll get the same!"

Four Dusters amused themselves by tormenting the ameboid. They turned the colloidal creature around on its casters and feinted blows to its plexi tank.

Dance said, "Why do these humans hate aliens?"

"Because they're bastards," said Matthew. "Stand back." He advanced on the group harassing the ameboid.

"Stop that," he said.

They laughed at him. The Dusters knew what Matthew was, and they had a grudging respect for him, but they weren't about to back down in front of so many potential victims.

Applique Face poked Matthew in the back with his rod. "Stay clear, spacer. You don't care about these vegetables."

Matthew turned slowly. "You never know," he said. "Some of my best friends are fruit." Applique Face screwed up his face to laugh, and Matthew put his fist in it.

The Dusters howled with delight and ringed Matthew. He ducked two, kicked another in the groin, and retreated to the wall. A heavy rod caromed off the concrete millimeters from his ear. Out came the plasmer. The Dusters stopped as if paralyzed.

"He's got a *gun*," said one reverently.

"On Luna," said another.

"He could kill us," added a third.

Applique Face got up and rubbed his chin.

"What's your name, spacer?" he said.

"Matthew Lawton."

"The dipper man?"

"Yeah, when I'm not burning troublemakers."

The Dusters backed away, mesmerized by the plasmer and awed to be facing a famous sundipper. In moments they were all together by the tunnel entrance.

"Hey, dipper man; is it true what they say about you?" asked Applique Face.

"Every word."

"Zoom," he said with a respectful nod. The other Dusters echoed "Zoom" and quietly fled. In seconds there was no trace of them.

Dance wended her way through the crowd to Matthew's side. "You impressed them," she said.

"Don't I impress you?" he replied.

"More and more, Matthew." Something hard bumped his back.

"What?" he said.

It was the ameboid. "My Pro, thank you for your assistance. My name is Clive Carl Candro. I am at your service," it said.

Dance had a strange look on her face. "Is this alive?" she said.

"Indeed I am. And what, may I ask, are you? You resemble a human female, but your physiological readings are quite alien," said Clive Carl Candro.

"What she is isn't important," said Matthew. "You offered service. What can you do?"

"Provide information, I believe," said the ameboid. "The Beneficial Party has agents on Luna searching for you, Pro Lawton."

He was surprised. "How do you know?"

"I work in Tranquility Communications Center. I processed the link myself. You and your companion are very much wanted."

"How much?" said Dance.

The ameboid pivoted nervously on its motorized chassis. "If you are Mrs. Mackensen, then you are the one they want. A major Pro on Earth wishes to bring you back. They are willing to kill Pro Lawton in order to get you," it said.

Dance said, "Matthew, what do we do?"

He looked at the plasmer, still hanging loosely in his hand. "Go on," he said grimly. "We have things to do in Tycho Basin."

CHAPTER 20

The day Matthew ferried the *Aztec* to Icecube was a day of considerable excitement. The dippers had heard great things about the new Photech ship, and they lined the lounge viewports to see Matthew glide the big ship in. The *Aztec*'s size made for difficult berthing; it had to be moored at the freighter pylon. Matthew remembered this was the same berth the *Collins* had used, so long ago.

Rather than answer the same hundred questions over and over to each dipper, Matthew had Photech prepare a chip on the *Aztec*. Played on the two-meter holoid cube in the lounge, the chip provided all the information anyone could want about the new ship. Matthew went to the main shop to find Arne Dawlish while the chip held everyone else's attention.

"Hey, Arn," he called across the echoing room. "I want to check you out on the *Aztec*. Got time?"

"Would it make any difference if I didn't?" said Arne.

"No."

"Then let's go."

163

The chief mechanic approached the *Aztec* with open-eyed wonder. "Beautiful, beautiful," he said, running a hand over its glassy skin. "Conductivity?"

"As close to zero as human engineering can make it," said Matthew. "I fired a hand plasmer at the leading edge from one hundred fifty cm, and it glanced off. No mark."

"Hmm, I bet the Service is in on this stuff," said Arne, ducking under the drooping wingtip.

"It's supposed to be on the new W-class dromons," Matthew said.

Arne, his voice muffled by the bulk of the *Aztec*, swore with delight. "What kind of cells are these?" he exclaimed. "I've never seen anything like them!"

"Selenium tri-modes," said Matthew. "They're supposed to absorb a broader band of spectra, making it easier to pull a hundred percent."

"As if you needed help."

"Everybody needs help out here, Arne." Matthew and the mechanic met by the engine exhausts. "Just your standard enhanced-energy reaction engines," he said. Arne peered through the slots on the outboard vents.

"Solid chip function throughout," he said. "What about pumps and turbines?"

"There aren't any."

"How the hell does the coolant and fuel circulate?"

Matthew fished a chip from his pocket and plugged it into a wrist viewer he wore. A schematic of the engine appeared in the air above his arm.

"See, heat exchangers are imbedded in the skin of the ship. When they get hot, they draw the operating fluids from the tanks by convective capillary action," he said.

"What happens when the exchangers cool off?" said Arne.

"A set buried in the exhaust nozzle automatically kicks in." Matthew removed the chip.

Arne was convinced. "It's a marvel, Matt. With this
beauty, even I could be a dipper," he said.

"Think so?"

The mechanic's well-wrinkled face relaxed. Arne was
by far the oldest person on Icecube. He'd actually known
Dunphy, Momar, and other greats. His paternal influence
was accepted and admired.

"How deep do you intend to go?" he said.

"No deeper than necessary," said Matthew.

Arne folded his arms. "I may be an old fart, but I'm not
stupid," he said. "What're you trying to prove, Matt?
How indestructible you are? There's limits to man and
machine that'll never be crossed. There's something else,
too. Talk's been going around about you. Bad talk."

"Let 'em rattle," said Matthew. "It doesn't bother
me."

"I'm wondering how true some of it is. They say you're
aiming to breach the convection layer. Others say you're
looking for the Cool Zones. A few think you're plain
crazy since Gem was lost, and that you're still looking for
her."

Matthew grabbed Arne by the collar. A fierce, dangerous light ignited in his eyes.

"You want to hurt me, Matt?" said Arne calmly.
Matthew dropped his hands hastily and apologized.

"Want to know what I'm really doing?" he said. "Want
to know the truth? If I tell you, you may really think I am
crazy."

"Can't say till I hear," said Arne.

"I'm looking for the source of the Gift."

Arne looked at his shoes. "It ain't there," he said.

"You believe in it too?"

"Hell yes, I believe in what I see and feel, just like you
do!"

"Then what do you mean, 'it ain't there'?"

"There's nothing to find. Certain wavelengths in the solar spectrum contain the Gift. That's all," said Arne.

"Suppose I tell you I lost the *Bedouin* to the influence of an unknown energy field? It was live, Arne. It maneuvered in the photosphere to evade me, but I caught it and flew right through it!"

"Doesn't that tell you something? You almost got fried."

"It told me I was after big game, and I better have the best damn ship made if I'm going to catch anything."

"And what'll you do if you do catch the Gift? Sell it to the Transasters?" said Arne. "How much more money do you want?"

"It's not for money. It's for . . . knowing. I have to know. I want to understand what Gem and Rainbow knew before they died," said Matthew.

Arne got a faraway look in his eye and said, " 'And the Tree of Life was guarded by an angel with a flaming sword.' "

"What?"

"Nothing. Something I read once," said the mechanic.

Matthew carefully smoothed Arne's suit and squeezed his shoulder. "Don't worry, old man. The chase is the game. I may never bottle the Gift, but I have to try. I'm not afraid to try."

"If I were you, Matthew my lad, I'd be afraid of succeeding," said Arne.

Aztec's maiden flight was Matthew's twenty-ninth dip. He left Icecube with an entourage of curious pilots and station people trailing behind in pogos. The *Aztec* passed Mitch Vine's *Rabbit Punch* incoming. The shadow of the far larger Photech ship fell across the *Rabbit*. Vine accelerated out of it, then angrily demanded who the bloody barge-pilot was. Icecube Control told him, and he said no more.

Matthew found the *Aztec* handled well despite its size. Photech had incorporated power augmenters into the controls, so it required a bare flick of the wrist to corkscrew. He rolled the ship a few times, halted, and reversed direction. Very smooth. Very smooth indeed.

The following craft slowed as the edge of Mercury's shadow neared. *Aztec* flew on. Matthew no longer used the Fire Truck. He suspected it dampened more than the corona.

Arne Dawlish and Len Rackham held the pogo *Icecube 15* inside the penumbra. Rackham watched the *Aztec* diminish in the distance. He was almost bursting with pride.

"There goes the future of our business," he said.

Arne replied, "If that's the future, give me back the past."

Len didn't understand Dawlish's remark. He understood even less when Arne quit his lucrative position as Chief Mechanic and departed for Venera-Vostok.

Matthew was gone almost fifty hours. The Icecube staff made nervous jokes about how Lawton was enjoying a solar vacation in his new ship. The jokes ceased after the forty-eight-hour mark. Then an incoming dipper (Dezzy Harper: three hundred bmW) spotted the *Aztec*.

The Photech ship approached slowly, aiming for the sixth pylon. There were no obvious signs of damage on the exterior. The slick white surface of the *Aztec* reflected Icecube's navigation lights with perfect fidelity as it closed in.

Len Rackham called Matthew repeatedly on the comband. He received no answer until the *Aztec* was fifteen hundred meters from docking.

"I'm OK," said Matthew tersely. "Alert Arne and have a mech crew standing by in anti-R suits."

"Arne's gone, Matt. He left for Venus thirty hours ago," said Len. The open band hissed.

"Right," said Matthew. "Have the mech crew ready."

Aztec slid into its new mooring system effortlessly. Ordinary magnetic clamps wouldn't hold the silicon-resin skin, so special "soft" claws gripped the ship at specially made dimples.

Once moored, the docking cradle hauled the *Aztec* into the shop. Matthew cracked the cupola and slid down the anhedral edge to the shop floor. Six mechanics lumbered into view, dressed in heavy antiradiation suits. One dragged a decontamination hose, another an R-detector. They circled Matthew and swept the air around him for deadly particles.

"Normal," said Kressberg, the man with the detector. "Background radiation only." Matthew smiled a peculiar, lopsided smile. He shook Kressberg's thickly shielded hand.

When the all-clear was given, Len Rackham rushed in. "God Almighty, Matthew! Where've you been?" he said.

"Inside."

"The sun? How could you stay so long?"

"I made it."

"Made it where?"

"The convection layer." The mechanics gawked.

"Impossible!" said Kressberg.

"I did it. What's more, I found pockets there, in the interface between the photosphere and the convection layer. Cool pockets, trapped like air bubbles beneath a sheet of ice," said Matthew. Someone snorted something about fairy tales. "You don't believe me?" he said, still grinning off-center. "I spent twenty-four hours in one of the pockets. I wanted to see how stable they were. They're stable enough! Mine was a perfect ovoid, sixteen hundred km long, four hundred and fifty wide and two hundred km deep."

"What was this cool pocket made of? How could it withstand the tremendous heat and pressure?" asked Len.

"I don't claim to know the physics behind them—or the paraphysics, for that matter—but they're there. It was cool, Len, a few thousand degrees Kelvin. The pocket was a field of energy. High stuff, much higher than I estimated. Higher than cosmic rays, Len. It was in a state of equilibrium. Somehow it achieved stability in the midst of the sun," he said. Matthew placed his hands on the station manager's shoulders. "I found the Gift, Len. I brought it back with me."

Two of the mechanics backed away and quietly fled. Rackham forced a smile and said, "That's quite a feat, Matt. How'd you do it?"

"Just by being there. I tried to draw the energy into the collectors, but it simply bled back through the walls of the cells. There's only one container capable of holding the stuff. The human body."

"You don't look any the worse for it."

"I'm not. In fact, I'm probably more alive now than I've ever been. You know, we've been all wrong about the Gift. It doesn't just enhance sexual potency; it strengthens every function within us," said Matthew. He faced the *Aztec* and crossed his arms.

"Rainbow tried to explain it to me. She searched many years for the ultimate secret. Her old, poorly shielded ship let hard rads in and she developed cancer four times over. But she didn't die! The Gift kept her alive. The tumors grew until they prevented her from making any more dips. She staved off death by taking the Gift from others—mostly Gem—until she was too weak and malformed. Slowly she lost the surcharge of energy. Not much penetrates Icecube. When the Gift faded, so did her protection. The cancers won out in the end."

As Matthew delivered this one-sided colloquy, Len Rackham quietly activated his intrastation com-band chip.

He whispered five words into the chip. Matthew did not hear him.

"Gem was searching, too, but in the wrong place. When I told her how I was going deeper toward the convection layer, she tried to beat me there. The *Topaz* was old. The tidal force must've pulled it to pieces before Gem could find the cool pockets," said Matthew. He hadn't spoken of Gem since his fight with Vine. The image of her face came back to him, and tears began to flow. They were the first he had shed for her.

Two medics appeared. Len waved for them to stand still. They loaded two dermo-dispensers with Crux and waited for the manager's signal.

"I feel the power within me, but I don't know what to do with it. It's like having too much money; it seems great until you have it, then you wonder what can you do with it? I thought the Gift might change me, make me think differently. All I feel is . . . alive. Very, very, alive," said Matthew.

Rackham jerked his head. The medics ran at Matthew's blind side. He heard their plastic soles scuffing on the floor and turned to face them. The nearer medic made an overhand thrust with his dermo-dispenser. Matthew blocked his attack. The female medic slipped behind him and jabbed the Crux into Matthew's midriff. He felt the sting and raised his hand to smash the medic across the jaw. When he saw her cringe back, he paused. The male medic was frightened of him too.

Matthew plucked the empty dispenser from his side. "Why, Len?" he said.

"You're having a breakdown, Matt. Have you heard what you've been saying? Cool zones, life-energy, life extension—a lot of nonsense. You need help. You need rest, and we're going to see you get some."

The woman had injected five cc's of Crux. Matthew's

extremities tingled, but the numbing blackness of the drug didn't seize him, even after several minutes. The medic picked up her empty dispenser.

"He's had a full dose and he's still standing," the medic said with awe. Rackham peered into Matthew's eyes.

"Are you on something?" he said. "Sting, maybe?"

"It's the Gift," said Matthew. He swayed slightly but kept his footing. "Do you think I'm crazy, Len?"

"Not crazy. Burned out. You've been dipping now for what, eleven quarters? That's a hell of a long time to spend in the sun," said Rackham.

Matthew took the second dispenser from the male medic. It also held five cc's of Crux. "I guess I ought to take this," he said.

"No!" said the woman. "You'll O.D.!"

"Not likely. I have the Gift, remember?" said Matthew. He stuck the drug pack to his forearm. The vacuum-loaded dispenser emptied instantly into the muscle.

The pack fell. The medics caught Matthew under the arms and lowered him carefully to the floor.

"Just goes to show you," Matthew mumbled.

"What?" said Rackham, but Matthew was out. "Take him to the clinic," said the manager. "Give him a thorough decontamination."

"The detectors show no radioactivity from Pro Lawton," objected Kressberg.

"Do it anyway. A man doesn't get five milliliters of Crux and not even yawn. Something was holding him up. Whatever it was, I want it washed out of him. Understand?"

The medics made assent and carried Matthew away. Kressberg and the mechanics went about their duties, taking down the *Aztec* after its flight.

Len Rackham stood back and gazed up at the shining white bulk of the ship. What had it and its pilot been through? He had heard the truth from Matthew, but could not comprehend it.

CHAPTER 21

The surface bus to Tycho Basin rolled quickly along the plexi-covered tube road. The only sound of its passage was the *whirr* of the wheels and the *whisk* of the induction plate below the motor on the power strip running down the center of the tube floor. The seats were full as usual, and Matthew stood so that Dance might sit.

"I can stand too," she said.

"I don't mind," he replied. Matthew wasn't being archaically gallant. If he was a target of Party agents, he wanted to be alert and on his feet should any danger present itself.

He fingered the plasmer in his pocket. Word would spread from the terminal about the spacer with a gun. There was no sterner prohibition on Luna than the antigun law. Possession of a weapon could earn the owner a life sentence in the gasworks on Bast.

They bisected Mare Nubium at a steady 110 kph. A few private vehicles passed them, going south to Tycho or

Pitatus. These were Earth people, as Lunarians were too poor to own cars. They packed the buses. Only Selenites used skimmers.

The bus stopped briefly on the outskirts of Guericke. Half the passengers filed off, but were promptly replaced by new ones. Most of the Guericke people were pharmaceutical workers on their way to the new Selenica plant. The spheres and spires of the factory glowered darkly over the crater roof. Matthew's father had built this one too.

The bus moved out from the Guericke station, gaining speed as the motor flywheel picked up momentum. The press of riders was so great Matthew was barely able to keep his footing as the bus swayed around Guericke offramps. After one sharp curve a figure clad in white thrust between Matthew and Dance.

Something hard and shiny was pressed into Matthew's side. The woman in white said, "Stay very still, Mr. Lawton."

"The Party," said Dance. Matthew didn't need to be told.

"What do you want?" he said. His hand strayed to his pocket.

"It would be very easy for me to kill you," said the Party agent. "This injector holds ten milligrams of Sarin, and if I squeeze it, you'll be dead before you can get your plasmer free."

"Relax," said Matthew as calmly as he could. "There's no reason for trouble here."

"Oh, I agree," said the woman. "All I want is your companion, Mrs. Mackensen."

"Tell Pro Taylor she can have David's property," Dance said. "I renounce it. I never wanted it."

"Taylor? What does District Chairman Taylor have to do with anything?" said the agent. "I'm with the Cooperation Chapter. My orders come from Atlanta."

Matthew swore inwardly. The Cooperation Chapter was the Beneficial Party's counterintelligence bureau. Very little was known about it, except that its attentions were unpleasant.

"If not for Pro Taylor, why do you want Sasha?" asked Matthew.

"You'll find out," she said, "if I decide to tell you." Pitatus Terminal loomed above them. "We're getting off here. I'll have the injector on you or Mrs. Mackensen at all times. Don't try anything stupid."

The rush of disembarking passengers wasn't heavy enough for Matthew and Dance to lose the Party agent. She stayed on Matthew's back right down the platform.

"Any luggage?" she said.

"We sent it ahead by freight express," said Matthew.

"Straight through the tunnel," said the agent. "Move."

Pitatus has a large nonhuman enclave. The Chapter agent and her captives waded into a large herd of Anubans who had just arrived from Deslandres. Matthew deliberately trod on the toes of a male Anuban.

"Pardon me," he said, stooping to help the creature back on its four feet.

"It is nothing, Mister," said the Anuban. Matthew peeked under his arm at the waiting agent. A faint glint revealed the injector hidden in the palm of her right hand.

"Did I break anything?" he said to the Anuban.

"No, Mister. Thank you for your concern."

The agent looked away for a moment. That was enough. Matthew shoved Dance aside and grabbed the woman's wrist. Dance sprawled on the pavement, scattering Anubans. The agent chopped at Matthew's throat, but he twisted his back to her and clamped both hands around the lethal injector. She pummeled his back with her free hand. Matthew wrenched her wrist. The strength faded from her fingers, and the injector dropped out.

Dance reached for it. "Throw it away!" yelled Matthew. Dance made to toss the device under the Gauricus bus, but a man in fashionable Ad-bans appeared and seized her by the neck and waist.

The woman agent jammed a leg between Matthew's and tripped him. She gave him a brutal kick in the ribs that crushed the breath from his lungs. He rolled up in a defensive ball. Another kick was primed and ready for his skull when some Pitatus constables appeared. The Chapter agent fled, following close behind the man who still held the feebly struggling Dance.

A Lunarian policeman helped Matthew to his feet. "What's the problem here?" he said. "Are you all right, spacer?"

"Yeah, yeah," said Matthew. He coughed. Blood flecked his fist.

"You need a medic. I think you busted a rib," the constable said.

"I'll live. Did you see two Earth people, a man and a woman, leaving the terminal?"

"No. Are they the ones who dusted you? Want them tacked for charges?"

The last thing Matthew wanted to do was go before a Lunarian magistrate and explain the truth about Sasha Mackensen. "No, no," he said. "It was my fault. The crowd was so thick I got pushed down. Somebody stepped on me. Now I just want to find my friends."

The Lunarian looked skeptical, but he clearly knew his own life would be less complicated if he went along with Matthew's story.

Matthew had one more question. "Where's the nearest spaceport?" he said. The policeman pointed to a holoid sign glowing overhead: GAURICUS. Matthew thanked him and moved on.

His rib throbbed unmercifully, and each breath was like a knife jabbed in his chest. He bought a handful of cheap painkillers from a vending machine. Popping them one by one, he joined the line for the Gauricus bus. If the Chapter agents were planning to take Dance back to Earth, that's where they'd go. And that's where he'd intercept them.

The bus filled up before Matthew's place in line got him on. Rather than wait for the next coach, he slipped the operator an extra decalot and sat on the steps below the operator's seat.

The bus made good speed on the Pitatus Overchange. Each time they passed a private vehicle, Matthew stood in the door and examined the occupants. Twenty minutes out of the terminal, the bus came alongside a dark green Tarantella, a powerful eight-wheeled machine. Matthew saw a flash of white in the windscreen. The driver turned her head and their eyes locked. It was the female Chapter agent.

The Tarantella zoomed ahead and cut sharply in front of the bus. The operator tapped his brakes and cursed the insolence of wetfoot drivers.

"What's the next road off?" Matthew asked the operator.

"The Gauricus Underchange," was the reply.

"And where in Gauricus is the spaceport?"

"East of town, on the plateau," said the Lunarian.

Fifteen minutes later the bus coasted to a halt. Matthew stepped down from the coach. He felt hot and nervous, a result of too many pain pills. But his rib had stopped throbbing, at least for a while.

Gauricus's main industry was magnesium mining and refining, and the air under the crater roof was tinged with chemicals and ozone. Endless trains of white metal ingots clattered east to the spaceport. Despite stern warning signs (ABSOLUTELY NO RIDING!), Matthew hopped on a magnesium carrier for a lift up the plateau.

The grade was steep. From the high ground east of the

crater Matthew could see the entire city. Sixty thousand people lived under Gauricus's roof. The high-rise multiminiums rose from the crater floor twelve hundred meters to the dome. The upper halves of these megastructures were uninhabitable; near the roof, the air was too thin.

The train topped the rise. The spaceport spread out fan-wise across the plateau. Great mushroom-shaped freighters packed with magnesium squatted on the fused lunar soil, poised to carry their cargoes to Earth, Mars, or points extrasolar.

On the southern perimeter of the port were the pogo pads. Matthew jumped from the train. The pogos were indistinguishable. They could be anyone's, going anywhere. He looked for the Tarantella. There couldn't be two machines like it around.

He moved cautiously among the fuel tanks and idle cargo handlers. One hand remained in his pocket, in reassuring contact with the plasmer. After passing a dozen pogo pads, Matthew spotted the dark green Tarantella parked ten meters from a boxy gray pogo-for-hire. There was no sign of the two agents or Dance.

Matthew crept to the rear of the vehicle. He drew the plasmer. Slowly he reached out for the door release panel. The door rolled noiselessly under the car. Matthew thrust his arm, gun first, inside.

"Matthew," said Dance.

She was free and unfettered in the rear seat. Draped across her knees was the unmoving body of the male agent who abducted her.

"And I thought you needed help," he said. "What happened?"

Dance cast her eyes down and said, "I was hungry."

"Is he dead?"

"Yes. It was wrong of me to drain him completely," she said. She let the body slip down to the floorboards. "His name was Ron."

"So what? He and his kicking friend were taking you back to be dissected or vivisected or God knows what. He got what he deserved." Matthew remembered they weren't clear yet. "Where's the woman?" he said.

Dance replied, "Arranging passage. She has been gone a long time."

"Then let's go. We still have to get to Tycho."

Dance climbed out of the vehicle. No sooner had she and Matthew stood up than they heard the female Chapter agent call out.

"Lawton! Mackensen! Stay where you are!" she cried.

He didn't think; he reacted. The plasmer came out and fear or drugs pulled the trigger. A shot flared off toward the sound of the woman's voice. The bolt splashed fire as it ricocheted on the hardpan. Dance exhaled sharply and fell to her knees.

"Hold your fire! There's fuel all around us!" said the agent. Matthew spied her. She and three Lunarians (probably the pogo's crew) were crouched behind an ingot stacker.

"Keep back and I won't shoot," Matthew yelled. Dance clutched his leg and reminded him of how the plasma discharge hurt her.

"Where's Ron?" called the woman.

"He's chilled. We're getting out of here, and you'd better let us."

"Can't do that, Lawton. Do you know what you've got? Your little friend is an alien, Lawton. A totally unknown species."

He muttered to Dance, "Get in the car." She crawled into the front passenger seat. Matthew walked around the other side. The agent and her hirelings stood out from concealment.

"Did you hear what I said?" the agent said. She pushed her light brown hair back from her eyes and flexed her fingers as if preparing for a fight. "The Chapter wants

Sasha Mackensen for evaluation, and I mean to have her!"

Matthew's hand strayed to the driver's door release. "Then the only thing to do," he said, "is kill you." He touched the opener and the door fell. He squeezed off a bolt at the agent and dived into the Tarantella.

How did this damn thing start? The steering control was a yoke, not a wheel. He grasped it. The dashboard lit up.

"Good," said Dance. "Let us go, Matthew. They are coming."

They were indeed. Armed with assorted blunt instruments, the Lunarians approached the vehicle from three sides. The woman hung back, fiddling with her toxin injector.

"Matthew, make the machine move," said Dance nervously.

"I'm trying, I'm trying!" The yoke moved on all four axes. Pulling back accomplished nothing. He pushed forward, and the Tarantella lurched into motion. A slow Lunarian was scooped onto the bow of the vehicle. He slid off when Matthew hit the plateau downramp.

The Chapter agent rounded up her confederates and ran for a low-slung ingot-carrying truck. Matthew saw them piling in as he tore down the ramp.

"We're in like Grynd," he said. "This go-car can outrun a truck any quarter."

"I hope so, Matthew. That woman is a pitiless character. She will kill you if she catches us," Dance said.

"I know." He pushed the yoke further in.

The Tarantella reached the Overchange. Holoid images pointed the way to Tycho Basin. Speed seemed more important than stealth, so Matthew turned directly onto the Tycho tunnel road exit.

Warning, said a letter display on the dash. *Overchange requires a higher motor conductor setting.*

"Well?" Matthew said to the car. "Where's the damn switch?"

"I see them!" said Dance. The truck was half a kilometer behind.

"Christ, where's the conductor setting?" he said. If they reached the Tycho tunnel without changing to the proper setting, their motor would stop. That would be the end of everything.

The control board flickered with a score of multicolored L.E.D.s. Matthew looked frantically from the road, to the dash, to the truck. Two hundred meters to the Tycho exit.

Dance held her left hand in front of the panel. She moved it in slow circles until her index finger paused over a blinking green L.E.D. Impulsively she pressed it, and it changed to blue.

Thank you, said the car's readout. *Conductor setting on automatic.*

"Thank God," said Matthew, squeezing Dance's hand appreciatively.

They merged with the southbound tunnel traffic. Moments later the truck appeared, weaving through the clots of slower vehicles. The gap between the Tarantella and the truck closed. Matthew had the yoke almost flush with the dash, but their speed would not go higher than 135 kph.

"They must have a damper on this thing," he said. "Or else the tunnel has a fixed-speed limiter."

The truck was still gaining. If evasion wasn't feasible, something more would have to be done. Something drastic.

"Think you can drive this thing?" asked Matthew.

"I have never— Is it necessary?" replied Dance.

"It is if you want to live."

"How can we exchange places? There is no way to stop."

"We'll do it on the fly. Put your hand on the center of the yoke and keep it pushed in." Matthew kept steering as he lifted his feet and tucked them under his butt. "Now, slip under my arm and sit on the floor." Dance wriggled into position.

"Put your hands under mine; that's right. You're going to have to steer. Just keep the studs on the wheel wells aligned with the red lines on the tunnel wall."

"I-I shall try, Matthew."

He released his hold and the Tarantella swerved drunkenly. Dance tried to compensate, and the left wheels scraped the concrete median.

"Steady!" he hissed. Dance nodded mutely.

He leaned over the seat and fell heavily into the rear. Ron was still there. Matthew found himself nose to nose with the corpse. The agent's eyes were rolled back and his tongue protruded. Matthew draped his jacket over the dead man's face.

The truck was barely fifteen meters behind. The operator and the woman were crammed in the tiny cab, while the other two Lunarians clung to the back of the open vehicle.

The rear window of the Tarantella was a solid sheet of plexi, slanting from the roof to the motor compartment. It had no release. Matthew pounded on all four corners, but the mounting held firm.

"Brace yourself!" he warned Dance.

He put the tip of the plasmer against the plexi, covered his face, and fired. Dance's head snapped back. The car slowed. She recovered and shoved the yoke in again.

A thirty-cm hole was melted in the window. Their pursuers saw the flash and slewed out of the way of the presumed bolt. Matthew waved the plasmer through the hole to warn them off. He saw the truck operator gesticulate, and the woman shaking her head. She would not be dissuaded.

"Matthew," said Dance. He tightened the stem for the smallest possible diameter bolt.

"Matthew!" she said sharply. He turned. "The tunnel is beginning to curve. What shall I do?"

"Stick to the inside lane," he said, "but don't slow down!"

As the surface road descended the Gauricus plateau, a series of S-curves were constructed to lessen the downgrade. Dance gazed at the serpentine course fearfully. She settled deeper into the seat and gripped the yoke tighter.

The Tarantella hit the first curve at 135 kph. Dance overcontrolled, and they skidded into the left lane. Matthew cracked his head on the roof. He swore violently, even though he hardly felt it past the pain pills. Hardly had he recovered from the first jolt when the opposite curve flung him to the right side of the car. He looked ruefully at the back of Dance's head. It was no use yelling at her; she was doing her best.

The Lunarian was a better driver, and he made up ground by cutting across the wide turns Dance made. In another two or three turns they would be alongside.

Matthew fired desperately. The bolt hit the top of the cab and blew it away. The truck nearly overturned, but the operator fought the controls and kept his machine upright. The next thing Matthew saw was the Chapter agent and the truck driver fighting in the cab. The Lunarians banged into the median. One of the men on the back fell off. The driver joined him, assisted by the toe of the woman's foot. At their present speed the Lunarians made a sickening splash when they hit the pavement.

Matthew swallowed hard and squinted along the flared stem of the plasmer. He aimed at the truck's wheelbase. The shot was intended to ruin the drive train. Instead the plasmer bolt hit the polished road surface, bounced, and struck the underside of the truck. The motor conductor exploded.

The agent wrenched the steering wheel hard left. The truck's wheels left the road and it began to roll. Four times, six, eight—with high-voltage current arcing from the road strip to the metal frame of the truck. The wreckage smashed into the concrete wall on the outside of a curve and halted.

The Tarantella slowed. Matthew said, "Don't stop."

"Should we give assistance?" asked Dance.

"No one could've survived. If we stop, we'll have to answer to the local constabulary. Drive on."

Dance eased the yoke forward. She and Matthew did not speak again until they reached Tycho Basin two hours later.

CHAPTER 22

They washed Matthew and hung him out to dry. He regained consciousness sick and sore, for the Gift had been wrung from his body by a barrage of drugs, filters, rinses, and solvents. Matthew was clean. Matthew was empty.

He never mentioned the Cool Zones to Rackham again. In fact, he said little to anyone. As the faces he knew were lost and replaced by ever younger dippers, his sobriquet changed. No longer was he Old Hundred Percent. Now he was the Silent Man.

The new dippers, cut off from him by a wall of silence, turned to other veterans for guidance and advice. Mitch Vine gathered a small band of admiring youngsters, and under his influence their opinion of Matthew was not kindly. Lawton was too famous, too powerful to openly confront—so far. Vine's protegés Dory Factor and Saburo Fuchida bided their time. Matthew was teetering on an edge and bound to fall sooner or later.

His bank account swelled to monstrous proportions as

he found less and less to spend his money on. His house on Earth was perfect; the *Aztec* was perfect; and Sian didn't want Matthew's money. She wanted to earn her own luxuries, not owe them to someone else. He approved of this sentiment.

Their love affair began to wear thin. Sian lived for ambition, and it suited her taste. Her position at Photech grew loftier, which whetted her appetite for more. While Matthew longed for simplicity and serenity, Sian dreamt of promotions. Their conversation evaporated as their minds no longer meshed.

Yet they remained intensely attached. Reunions on the mountain were always marathons of emotion, culminating in sex. The need was in both of them, but their hearts were no longer together. Matthew was unhappy going on. Sian was afraid to stop.

This was the state of things in the fourth quarter of Concordat Year 135. It was time to dip the sun, and Matthew prepared the *Aztec* for his thirty-third run.

How strange, he thought as he descended the lift from his tiny room to the lounge. To be in the most familiar place I know and not recognize anyone present. Dezzy Harper was gone, as were Fishman, Shapiro, Yates . . . Arne Dawlish was retired, and Len Rackham had gone out to Mars to be a gentleman farmer.

He crossed the lounge without acknowledging the stares of the idle clientele. At twenty-nine, Matthew had seven years' seniority on most of them. His weight was down to seventy-eight kilos. Hard red skin encased his frame like tooled boot leather. When Matthew looked in a mirror, he saw an eerie replica of Jack Sangamon.

Aztec was polished and ready to go. The crisply professional shop crew inserted him in the module and closed the cupola.

"Number thirty-three," he said as he activated the on-board audion.

"Beg your pardon?" replied the machine, still unnamed.

"This is my thirty-third dip."

"An enviable accomplishment in the field, sir," it said. "Have you set a numerical goal to attain before you retire?"

"Who said anything about retiring?"

"When one has as much success in a dangerous career as you have, sir, I thought it would be wisest to retire at some point to enjoy the fruits of your labors," said the audion.

He wondered where the machine had acquired its peculiar vocabulary. "Who made you my guidance counselor?"

"I endeavor to give good advice, sir."

"Tell you what: give me a good tangential course into the photosphere," said Matthew. "Leave the career planning to me."

The *Aztec* made a swift and efficient sweep of the photosphere. The cells were brimming when the audion reported an anomaly in the seething nuclear cauldron surrounding the ship.

"What sort of anomaly?" asked Matthew.

"I have a definite contact with an endothermic mass, four thousand eight hundred seventy-two km from the ship, on heading C–one hundred twenty one–seventy seven," it said.

"Composition?"

"Unable to determine in the massive background input. I would estimate it is a field of energy."

Ah, yes. He checked the density meter. He was thousands of kilometers from the convection layer, but he knew the pockets of energy that were the Gift sometimes penetrated the interface and rose through the photosphere.

"Track it," he ordered.

"Not necessary," said the audion. "It is not moving."

Matthew closed the collection array and steered the *Aztec* toward the anomaly. The range shrank to less than one thousand km.

"I discern a definite configuration," the audion said. "The mass is cylindrical, with the vertical axis pointing to space. The field extends coreward to the convection layer as far as my instruments can detect."

"How big is it?"

"The diameter varies from eight hundred seventy to one thousand one hundred twenty km. Is it your intention to approach this field?"

"No, I know what it is. Just curious."

Curiosity led Matthew to fly nearer the top of the anomaly. A holoid simul showed the field rearing up through the photosphere like a chimney. The audion described it as endothermic. The field was thousands of degrees Kelvin cooler than the gasses around it.

The *Aztec* pitched forward and down. Matthew snatched the controls hard back. The ship shivered under the opposing stresses and continued to dive.

"What the hell's happening?" he demanded.

"Differences in temperature have created a strong convection current around the anomaly. This condition is highly similar to the solar convection found—"

"Shut up. I know what you mean. Can we pull out of it?"

"Checking. No, sir; insufficient engine thrust. I recommend we accede to the pull and conserve fuel."

Simple enough. Matthew gave *Aztec* its head. Down they went, corkscrewing slowly. He could tell when they passed into the cool area because the heat-shielded instruments blipped on. The ship's momentum slackened, and Matthew took control once more.

"Forward motion zero. Vertical motion, down point four meters per second," reported the audion.

"Hold us level," said Matthew. He watched the dark module interior for signs of energy infiltration. There was nothing to see, but plenty to feel. The familiar tingle cooled his face and feet. The two tides flowed together in his abdomen. The Gift was back.

"I've missed you," he said aloud.

"Sir?"

"Nothing. Plot a course out through the top of the chimney. If the currents are circling the field, the force should be neutral if we exit along the central axis."

The sound of the engines whispered huskily from the rear of the module. The audion said, "Applying vertical thrust."

Aztec climbed slowly through the column. Bluish sparks collected on the consoles and controls. They danced and sparkled around the interior. Matthew laughed at them. They gathered at his face, as if trying to find the source of the sound he made. He laughed again, and the sparks scattered to the corners of the compartment.

"Sir? Sir?" said the audion.

"What?"

"There is a large metallic object outside the ship, sir."

Matthew snapped alert. "Where? What is it?"

"Heading A–twenty–three hundred forty-four. As to what, it seems to be a spacecraft of some sort."

"Ahead slow. Give me a display," he said. The cube came on. The exterior view was nothing but blue fire and brush discharges from the hull. Against this fluorescent backdrop, the audion painted a 3-D image of a derelict. It was small and circular, no doubt a dipper ship. But whose? How long had it been there?

"Can you increase the resolution? I want to see any hull markings there might be," Matthew said.

"A moment, sir; I will enlarge the image."

The derelict leaped nearer. Large gaps could be seen in

the ship's skin. It had been in the Cool Zone long enough for fatigue and corrosion to eat away the metal.

"I'm coming around," said Matthew. "Let the view pan." *Aztec* swung past the wreck's starboard side. Four exhaust cones showed. Matthew bit his lip till blood came. The craft was a Harvester type.

"Enhance detail," he said. The audion complied as well as the massive interference would allow. Matthew could make out seams and vents. The dorsal registration number had eroded to illegibility.

"How long would you say it's been here?" he asked the audion.

"I have no data by which to judge the rate of deterioration. However, no Harvester-type craft have been in active use since 133 c.y."

"Two standard years," Matthew said under his breath. *Aztec* rounded the lost ship's stern. As it passed, the derelict wobbled from its nose-down position. The port edge dipped and the whole wreck executed a slow tumble.

"What's wrong?" said Matthew.

"Our wake has upset the equilibrium that kept the craft in place. It is rotating and descending at an increasing rate."

"Can we stop it? I'd like to salvage it."

"We have no towing hawser, sir, and no reserve of power for pulling another ship. It is lost. It will spiral down and be taken by the convection layer."

Matthew steered *Aztec* after the falling ship. Harvester-class sundippers usually carried a nameplate on the hull aft of the cupola. Matthew had to know what ship this was.

"Listen," he said. "I want you to snap pictures of the wreck, behind the pilot's module, every time it rotates by us." The audion proceeded to reel off nearly a hundred holoid stills. Then Matthew let the ship go. It plunged ever faster through the thundering aurora until it disappeared from the instruments.

In open space Venus shone like a jewel, far off in the tactile black. Matthew felt surprisingly well. The Gift coursed within him as strongly as ever, and he had ninety-four still pictures of the derelict to study. As he headed back to Icecube, he ordered the audion to put them on the cube.

Most showed nothing but edges or the belly of the ship. On one turn, the camera did catch the cupola. The rear of the bulged lid was gone, disintegrated. The nameplate wasn't visible. He searched on, through fifty-odd frames, till he came to still No. 61. Slashing across the view was the rectangular nameplate. Only the last two letters were legible: —*AZ*. As in *Topaz*.

After that the nightmares began.

CHAPTER 23

They abandoned the Tarantella in a parking pit below
Leverrier Circle. The disheveled pair rode a conveyor to
Lowell Plaza. Matthew stepped off the track and doubled
over in pain.

"Are you all right?" asked Dance.

"That damn rib," he wheezed, clutching his side. "I
need a medic bad."

"If we can find a quiet place, I may be able to help,"
she said. He saw a nearby shopfront marked Blue Sky
Airfilters, Inc. Matthew gestured from his bent posture.

"There. There." He staggered forward. Dance followed so closely she trod on his heels.

The outer door parted for them. Matthew and Dance
crossed an empty hall to a lavatory. Inside, he collapsed
on the harlequin-patterned floor. He rolled over on his
back and stared at the softly glowing ceiling.

"You have much pain?" she said.

"Hell yes."

Dance used her index finger to find the nerve sending the pain impulse to his brain. So sensitive was her empathy, she could single out through many layers of muscle and skin the single strand of nerve fiber carrying the pain signals.

"It is here," she said, indicating a spot below his right breast. She pinched the seams of his shirt apart and slipped her cool hand under the cloth.

"What're you going to do?" he said.

"Impede the nerve so you have no pain."

Her fingers crept down, ignoring the beads of sweat trickling over his chest. Dance found the nerve locus and sent a jolt through it. Matthew's entire right side from the waist up numbed for a second, then returned to normal.

"That's great," he said. "How long will it stay blocked?"

"I do not know, Matthew. Perhaps a day."

"We're going to need money. If I can find a banking terminal, I'll withdraw as much as we'll ever need. Then I can get a meal and a bed for the night."

They left the Blue Sky building. Across the plaza they found a bank machine. Matthew withdrew two hundred kilolots. A credit chip popped out of the terminal.

"Right," said Matthew. "Food first and rest after. Sound all right?"

"I am hungry," Dance admitted. "But I doubt you can buy a meal for me." Matthew had an image of himself in a Lunarian eatery ordering rehydrated chicken for himself and a young man for Dance. No gravy, please.

Damn, I need sleep, he thought. In the hours since they landed on Luna, he'd fought, chased, and killed. Nerve block or no, he was exhausted. Dance seemed none the worse for her travail. She was used to living on the run. And this wasn't the first time she had been involved in killing.

They rode the conveyor to a good hotel Matthew knew of and checked in. Matthew lowered himself carefully onto a bed. An order of moo goo gai pan and a bottle of Sea of Dreams beer slid out of the room service panel. He ate. Dance sat on the floor in front of him and watched.

"Will the Cooperation Chapter continue to follow us?" she said.

"I don't know. With both agents chilled, they'll have a hard time finding us," he said. He dropped a chopstick. Dance retrieved it for him. "At any rate, we'll both be safe when we get to Icecube."

"I am not convinced that is the best course for me. Are you certain I can live on this Gift of yours?"

He took a long drink of beer. "No, I'm not. That's why we have to go by Tranquility University. I want to check on some references. Then we'll know."

They rested some hours. Matthew awoke and found Dance asleep on the tiled floor of the bathroom. Without bothering to wash or change clothes, they set out for Tranquility University.

It confused Dance that the university was not in the Mare Tranquilitatis. Matthew explained the discrepancy.

"Tycho is the principal Earth enclave on Luna," he said. "Since humans first set foot on Luna in the 'Sea of Tranquility,' the Earth people decided to honor the memory of those early explorers by naming their school after the landing site."

A wide, sedate conveyor carried them to the university. Along the way they saw a public news cube. A story blared about the shooting and wreck on the Tycho road. So far the constabulary were still seeking the green Tarantella.

The university was deserted. It was an interim period, and classes were not in session. Matthew and Dance went to the Von Braun Library. Far in the back, screened from prying eyes and ears, Matthew consulted the index. For quietude's sake, he set the computer for visual display rather than voice.

He entered: *Request reference locator.*

PROCEED read the display.

Find Od, he typed.

SPELLING CORRECT? Matthew indicated it was. CHECKING . . . OD: OD; DEFINITIONS. OFFICER OF THE DAY. ORBITAL DIRECTION. OVERDOSE. OVERDRAFT. The spherical cursor paused within the cube.

Any other references? asked Matthew.

NO OTHER REFERENCES: OD, O-D.

"What are you after, Matthew?" said Dance.

"Some data a friend once gave me. I want to see if I can find any info about the Gift in the library records."

He typed, *Find Vril.*

CHECKING . . . CROSS-REFERENCED TO BULWER-LYTTON, EDWARD: FICTION, NOVELS, TERRESTRIAL, PRE-CONCORDAT ERA 2, THE COMING RACE.

"What is that?" said Dance.

"A novel, I think." He entered, *Retrieve The Coming Race.*

HARD COPY CLASSIFIED RARE MOST VALUABLE. HOLOID COPY AVAILABLE.

Retrieve holoid copy.

RETRIEVING . . .

The cube grew smoke colored. A thick book, bound in green leather, appeared in the viewer. Matthew tapped the page-turn control. The phantom cover flipped open. Two flyleaves later, they reached the title page: *The Coming Race; Falkland, Zizzi, and Pausanius the Spartan.* London, Routledge, 1878.

"How old is this?" said Dance very quietly.

"Four hundred Earth years, give or take a decade or

two." It seemed impossible that a work from the Age of Impatience could contain any useful information on the Gift.

Matthew began to read. He did so aloud, because while Dance understood written Solarian, English was beyond her. The story told of men who went under the crust of the Earth and discovered a marvelous civilization, the Vril-ya, living there.

"Is this true?" asked Dance. "Do beings live beneath the surface of your world?"

"No, it's only a novel."

"Untrue? Why would anyone record an untrue story?"

"Entertainment. Humans like to read stories of things that never have or never could happen," he said.

In Chapter VII he found a clue. One of the surface men tried to explain what the strange force *vril* was. He said

. . . there is no word in any language I know which is an exact synonym for vril. I should call it electricity, except that it comprehends in its manifold branches other forms of nature . . . The people [the Vril-ya] consider that in vril they have arrived at the unity in natural agencies.

Later the narrator says of vril, "It can destroy like the flash of lightning; yet, differently applied, it can replenish or invigorate life, heal, and preserve."

"There, you see," said Matthew. "Sounds perfect for you."

"But you said this was not true."

"The events are fictitious. The facts may be—should be—true."

She was still doubtful, so Matthew returned to the index. *Find Orgone*, he typed.

CHECKING . . . THERE ARE ONE HUNDRED FORTY-FOUR DIS-

TINCT REFERENCES TO ORGONE IN THE INDEX. DO YOU WISH
FOR A COMPLETE LISTING?

"I think we just filled an inside straight," said Matthew.
Select reference by earliest date of publication.

CHECKING . . . CROSS-REFERENCED TO REICH, WILHELM:
MEDICINE, PSYCHIATRY, ARTICLES, TERRESTRIAL, PRE-
CONCORDAT ERA 1, "UEBER EINEN FALL VON DURCH-
BRUCH DER INZESTSCHRANK."

"Damn it!" *Select by title Orgone. Specify English/
Solarian text.*

CHECKING . . . THE DISCOVERY OF THE ORGONE: VOLUME I,
VOLUME II.

Retrieve holoid copy.

Matthew skimmed over many pages of the old medical
text. There were many terms he didn't understand, but
here and there sentences stood out like beacons. Gem
had been right; men of the past had known the Gift
well.

"Look at this!" he said. Dance bent closer over his
shoulder.

"Orgone is universally present . . . when visible, it
appears as a blue glimmer or gray-blue vapor . . . *sun
energy . . . energy of the sun condensed to solid
form.* . . orgone originates anywhere matter is heated to
the highest state of incandescence . . . the decay of matter is essential to its formation . . . living things absorb
from the atmosphere or from the sun itself.

"My God, we've found it," Matthew said. He read of
this Dr. Reich's experiments in collecting orgone for
study. The doctor had found that only organic substances
would retain the power; metal vessels reflected it away.
Living tissue was the best container of all.

Orgone killed cancer cells. It enhanced sexual potency. It did everything the fabled Gift was said to do, and
more.

"Do you believe me now?" he said. "Shall we go on to Icecube?"

In the pale green sheen of the computer cube, Dance looked very young. "Yes, Matthew, I will go if you make a pact with me," she said.

"What kind of pact?"

"That should this sun-vril, this orgone not be suitable to sustain me, you will return me to a place where humans live, uncontaminated by the Gift." Something else remained unsaid.

"And?" said Matthew.

"And you will not thereafter interfere with my feeding habits," she said.

Matthew agreed.

The corridors of Tranquility University were vacant. Dance and Matthew walked along the center of the main tunnel, Aldrin Hall.

"You were instructed here?" said Dance.

"Yeah, but I left without taking a degree."

"Why?"

"I wasn't learning what I wanted to know. They taught history and language and the physical sciences; I wanted to express myself."

She said, "Is that why you became a sundipper?"

"Dipping was a way to make a lot of money," he said. "Only later was it an end in itself."

They stopped at an elegant circular lecture hall. A public address cube two meters wide hung from the apex of the fluted vault ceiling, sending a null message to the empty seats.

" 'Sic transit gloria mundi,' " Matthew said in the open doorway.

"What does that mean?"

"School's out, come back next quarter."

Dance descended the shallow steps to the central podium. She mounted the dais. The podium lit up, and the cube overhead was filled by her image.

"On my world, we have gathering places where we come to learn," she said. Her voice was a scant whisper, yet it penetrated every square centimeter of the hall. "Those who know share with those who do not."

"Sounds fair. Earth people have a saying: 'Those who can't do, teach; those who can't teach, teach teachers.'"

"Matthew, why are you so dissatisfied?"

"Who says I am?"

"Since I have known you, there has been nothing in your mind but this need for finding. About me, the Gift, the fate of your loved one—"

"I thought you couldn't read human thoughts?"

"I cannot. What I know of you I have seen, or heard you speak in your sleep. The female, Gem. You often call to her. She is dead?"

"Dead and gone."

"And Sian? You have dismissed her?"

"Our relationship is over, if that's what you mean," said Matthew. "You're being awfully nosy. What're you getting at?"

"You and I, Matthew. We must define what we are. I suspect you think of me as a replacement for the females you have known, and this cannot be. My appearance is a deception."

"As you keep reminding me. So what? Does that mean we can't be friends? Does your race recognize friendship?"

"Of course. Cooperation is the bond between all Those Who Think."

"Then be my friend. That's all I expect."

Dance stepped down from the podium. Her face vanished from the cube, and her voice reverted to its normal timbre.

They had places reserved on the Venerian dromon *Tashkent*. Together they went to meet it.

CHAPTER 24

The delegation cornered Matthew in his cabin. Six leading dippers, plus an equal number of important station people formed the group. Dory Factor, Mitchell Vine's most successful protegé, was their leader and spokesman.

"You know why we're here," he said.

"Yeah, I'm sorry I wasn't around to see Mitch off, but he and I didn't exactly get along," said Matthew. Vine had left eight days ago. He was returning to Earth for medical treatment—bone marrow transplants. He had myeloid leukemia.

"That's not it," said Dory, though everyone recalled his anger at Matthew for not being present when Vine left.

"Then what the hell do you want?" Matthew said testily. The group had rousted him out of bed, and it was annoying to sit there facing them wearing only his Cooler mesh.

"You're the greatest dipper of our generation," said Dory, "and all of us respect your record. But when it comes down to the security and survival of the sundipping business, even Matthew Lawton has to give way to the general welfare of the industry."

"Speak straight, will you? You're giving me a head-ache."

"You've cracked," said Edmondson, a mechanic.

"Is that what you think? My nerve's as good as it ever was. Anyone want to test it?"

"We're not talking nerve," said Dory. "If anything, yours is too good. Weaker dippers would've flaked a long time ago. Not you. Not Hundred Percent Lawton. You'll dip till the sun burns out. But not here. Not with us."

"Who's going to stop me? I own the largest percentage of this station. My allotments are five times my nearest competitor's." He snapped to his feet. "And who the hell are you bastards to judge me? When did you get medical degrees?"

Dory retorted, "Look, Lawton, you've got to see things clearly. This talk of yours about the 'Gift' is getting out of hand. Our distributors have heard about it, and they want to cut prices. They're saying, if we derive so much benefit from this mysterious force, why should they pay so heavily for energy we'd collect for nothing?"

"And what's all this bullshit about Cool Zones?" said Fuchida, another pal of Vine's. "The new pilots hear that rot from an old pro like you and they believe it. Did you know a girl named Akeley fried herself in a spicule while looking for one of your damned zones?"

"Is it my fault she was stupid? Am I to blame for her being a third-rate pilot? I never told anyone to look for the Cool Zones."

Fuchida had wounded him deeply here. Matthew remembered Lauren Akeley, who at nineteen had all the boldness of a veteran without the skill. She died as Jack had, diving under a billowing spicule for the presumed safety of the Cool Zone. His guilt in her case was considerable.

"You're just off a good run," said Dory. "Why don't you quit early and go home for the rest of the quarter?"

"I have a contract to fill," Matthew said loftily. He was still the only dipper who made and filled specific contracts. "Besides, I don't take orders from a gang of white-skinned rookies."

"Too bad. You could've saved everyone a lot of trouble." With a flick of his head, Dory signaled the attack. He, Edmondson, Fuchida, and two others rushed Matthew. They bowled him over and pinned him to the cold metal floor.

"Get off! Let me go, you bastards!" he raged.

"Quick, Lia! Give him the stuff!" gasped Dory.

Matthew got a hand on Fuchida's throat and hurled him out of the pile. He jabbed Edmondson in the stomach and a man he didn't know on the jaw. Free of these obstructions, he was about to turn his attention to Dory Factor when a medic stuck a dermo-dispenser into his strained left leg.

He knew what it was: Crux. Five cubic centimeters of quick-acting comatic. He stopped struggling and laughed.

"I hope you have another," he said. "One won't put me under."

"Hold him, chases; he's being tricky," said Fuchida.

"Ha, ha, ha! You won't believe it, will you? The Gift exists. You all have it. I have it more, 'cause I know where it hides. It's a good friend of mine."

"He's raving," Dory said incredulously.

"He's drugged," corrected the medic, "but he's not going under."

"Get him up," said Dory. He and Edmondson grabbed Matthew by the arms and hauled him to his feet. Matthew shifted unsteadily from one foot to another.

"The old-timers knew about the Gift," he said. His lips felt furred, and his tongue adhered to the roof of his mouth. "Dunphy, Momar, Rainbow, Red Jack Sangamon; they all knew. You're fools! You chase each other around, fuck every willing body from here to Titan and *feel* the power, but you won't face the truth.

"The Gift is the power of God!"

"Give him another dose," said Dory.

"His heart may stop," said Lia, the medic.

"Are you kidding? He's strong as a Martian wrestler," said Fuchida. Lia held the dispenser to the light. She pressed the tab at the base and another five cc's of Crux filled the vacuo-vial.

"I'm against this," she said.

"Do it," said Dory.

"Yeah, do it," said Matthew. "The heart stops, the brain dies, but the light goes on forever."

Lia bent down. Matthew took her hand that held the dermo-dispenser and pulled it toward him. As the twin microbores pierced his skin, he looked unblinkingly into the young medic's eyes.

The effect was immediate, like a blow on the head. Matthew went limp and barely breathed.

The delegation surrounded him. Three of the men lifted him up and laid him across the rumpled bed.

"What do we do with him?" said Edmondson.

"Bring a sub-C hybernation box from the clinic," said Dory. "Pack him in and send him home."

This they did. Two medics stripped him, affixed sensors and life-support leads, and poured cold vitalyn gel into the box. The supply ship *Pendray* was outward bound, and the delegation slipped Matthew on board. They charged the shipping cost to Matthew's Icecube account.

CHAPTER 25

The *Tashkent* was delayed for thirteen hours by fueling problems. Matthew and Dance cooled their heels in McDivitt Receiving House. His rib throbbed dully as the nerve block began to wear off. Matthew put his feet up on a chair and stretched back to lessen the pressure on his side. He fell asleep in this position.

Pain awakened him. He coughed raggedly and felt something hot catch in his right lung. "Dance, I need you," he said. Dance was nowhere near. Matthew scanned the entire establishment and didn't see her.

Where could she have gone? Had another Chapter agent snatched her? Or was she out hunting a meal?

He accosted a baggage mover near the entrance. He described Dance and asked the Lunarian if he'd seen her.

"Ah, straightly! I give her directions," he said. "She wanted to find junk sellers. You know, Pro. Antykews."

Antiques. "Where'd you send her?" asked Matthew.

"Ptolemy Circle. Lots of junk dealers down there."

A brief conveyor ride later Matthew stood in Ptolemy Circle, one of the low-rent areas of Tycho. Antique and junk shops abounded (the difference between them was theoretical at best). He went door to door, asking after the Earth woman with long brown hair. The shopkeepers remembered her.

"That twitch?" said one ancient Lunarian. "She wanted to buy audio discs. Can you shake that dust? If I had audio discs, would I work in a cave like this?"

Matthew moved on. At least he knew what Dance was after. She found David Mackensen's old elpees so compelling, she was risking valuable escape time trying to find more.

He caught up with Dance in a place called Nicolai's Debris. The proprietor (Nicolai?) was arguing with her.

"I tell you, I ain't got any records 'cept what you see in the holoid. Just classicals—Mozart, Beethoven, and Tchaikovsky," he said.

"Can you get others?" said Dance plaintively. "Perry Como? Nat King Cole? Dean Martin?"

"Not unless a megalot collector decides to unload his collection on me. Move along, wetfoot; I don't want to see you no more," said Nicolai.

"Perhaps he'd be willing to buy your elpees," said Matthew, emerging from the dim doorway.

Nicolai squinted at him. "You got some to sell, spacer?" he said sharply.

"Maybe hers. My friend likes the music on them, not the discs themselves. Do you know where we can have the music transferred onto musicon chips?" said Matthew.

"Roddy Usher has all kinds of old electronic gear. Could be he can help you," said Nicolai.

"Where can I find dryfoot Roddy?"

Nicolai's lashless eyes flickered suspiciously. "Am I gonna get to see the goods?"

"If Roddy can rerecord for us, we'll come back," said

Matthew. Nicolai gave them an address on Mercator Lane. Matthew took Dance by the elbow and hustled her from the shop.

Outside Dance said, "Why did you tell him that? I don't want to sell the elpees."

"They'll be no good on Icecube," said Matthew in a low voice. "You need alternating current to operate the player, and all the systems on the station are technotronic. If you want to save the music, you'll have to get it put on chips."

Mercator Lane was a dirty, narrow passage six blocks from Ptolemy Circle. The ceiling was very low, and for the first time since arriving on Luna they felt truly underground.

Roddy Usher's shop was decorated with bits of archaic electronic equipment. Magnet-cone speakers, amplitude modulation receiving sets, and video viewers hung from wires overhead. Roddy Usher himself, a short, thin man as dry as lunar dust, constantly rubbed his hands together as he talked.

"Well, well, what distinguished customers," he said raspingly. "What can dryfoot Roddy do you for?"

"You can be of service," said Matthew. "Do you have equipment that can play Impatient Era recording discs?"

"Elpees? But of course. I have a very fine quadrophonic system in the back, with two channels still functional—"

"We don't wish to buy," said Matthew. "We want to translate the music from certain elpees onto standard musicon chips. Can you do that?"

Roddy scratched his pointed chin. "Hmm. It can be done, my Pros. I'll have to interface the output channels of the turntable with a techno-simulator . . ." The old Lunarian drifted in thought. "Expensive process, my Pros," he said.

"Ten decalots per chip," said Matthew.

"Twenty."

"Twelve."

"Eighteen?"

"Fifteen," said Matthew, "and not a millit more."

"Well, well, I s'pose I can do it for that," said Roddy. Dance handed over her treasured elpees. The Lunarian carefully unwrapped the static paper from the black vinyl discs. He held the elpees gingerly by the edges.

"Excellent, excellent," said Roddy. "I haven't seen such well-preserved elpees since I came to Tycho. Where'd you get them?"

"They were my husband's," said Dance. "He was a collector of old things."

Usher puttered about the cluttered shop, dragging out odd-looking metal boxes and long bundles of stranded copper wire. Soon he had a U-shaped array of equipment lashed together. He set the tone arm on the first elpee and began recording.

The process took hours, since the music could only be transferred at playing speed, not high speed as with chips. The time passed strangely as each song melted into the next, each record filling the shop with the voices and music of men long gone. All twenty-three elpees went into four chips. Matthew paid Roddy sixty decalots.

"Well, well," said Roddy, caressing the money chip in his small gray hand. He acted as if he had never expected to see the money promised to him. "Well, well! Do visit again, my Pros, and tell your friends about Roddy Usher!"

They hurried back to Nicolai. The *Tashkent* was due to take off in forty minutes. If they missed the proper departure window, Matthew and Dance would have to wait on Luna thirty-two days until Icecube was in range again.

Nicolai examined each disc with infuriating care. He wanted to haggle over the price. Matthew grew so impatient he seized the Lunarian by the sleeve and said, "Give us two kilolots for all twenty-three." The elpees were worth eight times as much.

"S-sure," said Nicolai. He coded a chip and gave it to Matthew. The latter pressed it into Dance's hand.

"This is your money," he said. "Let's go."

They ran from the shop. Nicolai watched them race for the upward conveyor.

"Wetfeet," he said with a shake of his head. He reached for the pile of recordings. His fingers stopped a centimeter from them.

"Stolen?" he mused aloud. He shrugged and tucked the rare old discs under his arm. Business was business.

The *Tashkent's* departure from Tycho was so rough Matthew seriously reinjured his rib. He coughed blood on his seat and gasped for air. The broken rib had finally perforated his lung.

The *Tashkent's* medician was a dour man of many years' experience. He injected Matthew with osteomax, reinflated his lung, and wrapped a heavy bandage around his chest. Matthew spent the rest of the journey to Icecube in his bunk. Dance hovered nearby. Her concern was divided between the both of them. Her hunger grew sharper by the hour, and if Matthew was unable to take her dipping soon after they arrived at the station, she might have to take drastic measures. Such as tapping a crewman on the *Tashkent*.

Matthew knew this. He could see the want on her face, and the intense looks she gave members of the dromon's crew.

"Hold out," he said. "We're cleanly away, and if you behave, we'll soon be free and clear." Then the pain lanced across his chest, and he fell back into agonized silence.

* * *

Mercury circles the sun once every eighty-eight Earth days. As the *Tashkent* slowed in the planet's path, Mercury raced to meet the Venerian vessel. Five days and eleven hours out of Luna, *Tashkent* kept its rendezvous with Icecube.

The Venerians off-loaded their cargo of low-bulk, high-value goods—audion parts, drugs, and magnesium ingots—directly into the station's shop. Matthew crossed the boarding tube on his own two feet. It was the first time he'd walked since leaving Luna. Dance offered to support him, but he shunned her help. He had left Icecube on his back. Returning, he would stand.

Anatoly Kressberg, now chief mechanic, was supervising the dispersal of the *Tashkent's* cargo. He heard slow footsteps and looked to see who was coming. Matthew and Dance emerged from a swirl of CO_2 vapor venting from the supercooled audion crates.

"Lawton!" he said.

"Kressberg," said Matthew. "How's the *Aztec*?"

"Uh—fully mothballed. The manager had it shrouded."

"Unshroud it. I want it ready to go in half a day. Clear?"

"Straight and clear," said Kressberg. The pair passed the mechanic and made for the lift to the lounge. By the elevator doors Matthew paused.

"This is my friend, Dance. Dance, this is Kressberg," he said.

"Hello," said the mechanic.

"Greetings," said Dance.

The lift arrived. Matthew and Dance entered it. Before the doors closed, Matthew announced, "Dance is my new apprentice. She's going to dip with me." The doors slid shut and smothered Kressberg's incredulous reply.

*   *   *

The lounge was well filled. Sunspots were rife, and the dippers were playing things cautiously, staying close to Icecube while the storms raged around the sun.

Matthew led Dance to a table along the far wall. They sat, facing outward. Every eye in the lounge was on them.

Four dippers appeared. Two Matthew knew—Dory Factor and Saburo Fuchida. They ringed the open side of the table.

"Back again, Lawton?" said Dory. "I thought you were taking a long rest."

"I'm rested. How's your health?" replied Matthew.

"Perfect. Things have been going pretty straight since you left." Dory leaned forward, resting his palms on the table. "I hope they stay straight," he said.

"Why shouldn't they?"

Fuchida said, "You were disturbed when you left, Pro, saying things that shouldn't be said. That's not going to happen again, is it?"

"What do they mean?" asked Dance.

"They mean the Gift," said Matthew. "It bothers them when I talk about it."

"Careful," said Dory.

"Why?" said Matthew, raising his voice. "Everyone here has heard of the Gift. Why not discuss it? Why don't we investigate it? As long as it was a dirty joke, nobody cared what was said. Why do you paleskins care now?"

Dory pulled the table away. Matthew stood. He was taller and faster than his opponents, but there were four of them, and his rib was still tender. Dance stood beside him.

"You didn't learn a thing last time, did you, Lawton? Your brain's been melted by too many deep dips," said Dory, holding his temper down with difficulty. "Life's tough enough out here without spacey old farts ranting about God and gifts and magical energy. You have a choice: be straight and do your job, or get retired."

"By you?"

"By us," said Fuchida.

"What a bunch of androids! The Gift is all around you, *in* you, and all you can think of is money and your reputations. I haven't survived fourteen quarters as a dipper and seen better men and women than you die to quit now," said Matthew.

He charged forward, arm outthrust. Dory and the unnamed dipper on his left lowered their shoulders and blocked Matthew's path. Fuchida shoved Dance aside and circled behind him.

No blows were exchanged, though the men struggled intensely for several seconds. Dance saw blood running from Matthew's lips.

"He is injured," she said, tugging vainly at Fuchida. "Let him go!" Factor tried to wedge his leg between Matthew's to trip him. Even hurt, Matthew was remarkably strong. He sent Dory's associate sprawling, and got a hard grip on Factor's upper arm. Fuchida wrenched Matthew's right arm back, and Matthew groaned as the injected osteomax on his rib gave way.

"Let him go!" cried Dance. She touched three fingers of her left hand to the back of Fuchida's neck. When firm contact was made, the dipper stiffened. Without a sound, he went rigid and fell face down on the floor.

Dory and Matthew separated. Factor knelt by his friend. Fuchida was alive, but paralyzed.

"What did you do?" Dory said to Dance.

"He was hurting Matthew. Can't you see he is bleeding?" she said. Matthew sagged to the floor near Fuchida, gripping his right side. Someone across the lounge yelled for a medic.

Fuchida was conscious. He blinked his eyes furiously at Dory, for this was the only voluntary movement he could make. Before the medics arrived, Dance helped Matthew to his feet. They hobbled together to the lifts.

Matthew faced the lounge. "I want everyone to know I'm not crazy. The truth exists whether you want to believe it or not. No one's in any danger from me or the knowledge I profess. Do your jobs, make your money; makes no difference to me." He coughed once, painfully. "Most of you will die out there, screaming into the roar. The best people I ever knew died in the sun. So have some of the worst. But remember this: if I disappear on my next dip, I won't have died in pursuit of money." He put an arm over Dance's shoulder. "That's all," he said.

In the elevator Matthew said, "What did you do to Fuchida?"

"I interrupted the motor nerve responses from his neck down," Dance said. "He will recover."

"I didn't know you could do that."

"Until it happened, neither did I."

No one harassed them again. While Kressberg brought the *Aztec* to flying trim, Matthew spent five days immobilized in his cabin. He ate and slept there, stretched out on his back. When the pain came, Dance blocked it for him.

She learned to sleep on the steel floor by his bunk. It made Matthew unhappy at first, her lying there. He didn't like her lying at his feet like some devoted pet. Dance explained that soft surfaces induced feedback in her highly sensitive sensory system, preventing her from resting. Matthew said no more about it. When his rib was healed, he took to sleeping on a pad beside her.

Dance adapted slowly to station life. Matthew cut her hair so she would fit the hood of her heatsuit. The short style revealed the one alien feature she hadn't been able to change: the bony crests that arced over the back of her skull. In time the hair would grow back. Until then, Dance had to wear her hood whenever she left the cabin.

No one suspected her of being anything other than Matthew's apprentice. Common gossip made them lovers as well, and Matthew did nothing to discourage those stories. The last thing he wanted was some itchy dipper trying to seduce the starving Dance before they dipped the sun together.

At last they stood side by side in the great shop, now nearly deserted as the other dippers resumed their trade. An odd pair they were. Matthew was leaner and darker than ever, while Dance resembled a cloth doll in her heatsuit. The *Aztec* loomed over them, ready and waiting.

"Time to go," said Matthew. "You ready?"

"I am prepared," said Dance.

He consulted his chronograph. "I'll be damned," he said. "I turned thirty two days ago and forgot all about it."

"Thirty is not an advanced age in humans. Does it have some social significance?"

Matthew dropped his wrist. "It's very old for a sun-dipper," he said with a smile.

They settled in the *Aztec* and left Icecube without incident. Matthew intended their first dip together to be routine. He set an easy parabolic course and made no attempt to penetrate the photosphere too deeply. Dance's entire future was riding on this flight. No sense taking unnecessary risks.

Aztec functioned perfectly, and only the alterations in instrument readouts betrayed their entrance into the sun. As they thrust inward, Matthew found himself gripping the arm of his seat tightly.

Come on, come on. I know you're there.

Risesunrisesunrise—

The Gift returned like an intimate friend, quiet and warm. It seemed to know Matthew, and it welcomed him. The struggle, the long deprivation was over. He felt deep satisfaction as the familiar aura saturated the module.

Here I am. Hurtling through the sun made all else seem petty and futile. All the vanities of the past weeks surfaced in Matthew's mind like dross in a crucible of molten gold.

His fear of insanity. Sian's insecurity. His own jealousy. His fear of Dance. His desire for Dance. The Beneficial Party and all its myrmidons. Dross. Ephemera. Atoms blown away on the solar wind.

And when his mind was free of unimportant things, Matthew understood as Rainbow had understood. The sun's pulse was his pulse. Through the clarity of the Gift, he knew again all those who had counted in his life. For good and ill, they were all there: his mother, father, and brother. Rangy Jack Sangamon. Len Rackham, Arne Dawlish, and even Wellington Yu.

Rainbow Harvester smiled at him with the unblemished face of a child.

He kissed Sian's cheek and said good-bye.

I love you, Gem, he thought, and she replied, "It is good to be loved." He realized she had never been lost; he'd lost himself.

"I came back for you," he said aloud.

"What? Are you well, Matthew?" asked Dance.

"Yeah. Do you feel it? The Gift?"

"Yes, Matthew. It is good."

Aztec reached the bottom of its course and began to climb out of the fire. The pure life-energy, the od, vril, orgone, filled them, overfilled, touched and flowed together. The woman who was not a woman, and the man who was yet a man, met in true communion, intermingled by the glorious gift of the sun.

The dippers and their craft emerged from the corona into open space. The light they carried went with them.

The Legendary Science Fiction Novel

THE SPACE MERCHANTS
by Frederik Pohl and C. M. Kornbluth

"A novel of the future that the present must inevitably rank as a classic!"   —*The New York Times*

___ __ 90655 2 $3.50 U.S.   _____ 90656-0 $4.50 Can.

And the Brilliant Sequel

THE MERCHANTS' WAR
by Frederik Pohl

"We've waited a long time...and our patience has been well rewarded."   —*Best Sellers*

_____ 90240-9 $3.50 U.S.   _____ 90241-7 $4.50 Can.